She was tiny.

Just a little over five feet, but her presence was impressive.

She had a compact body with curves he shouldn't be noticing. Her hair was short, too, with black spikes and curls framing a face that was heart shaped, with a full mouth, high cheekbones and green eyes that were bright and shining with eagerness. She wasn't at all what he'd been expecting.

Hannah Yates of Yates Construction.

"How soon do you need this done?" she asked, tossing him a glance over her shoulder.

"Four weeks."

"Hah!" She grinned, shook her head as if he wasn't making sense.

Shrugging out of her dark green hoodie stamped with *Yates Construction* across the back, she tossed it onto an overturned table leg. Then she shook her head and pushed one small hand through that short, black hair.

Something stirred inside him and he fought it down.

Hannah Yates was his last hope of getting the restaurant back up and running in time.

* * *

The Wrong Mr. Right by Maureen Child is part of the Dynasties: The Carey Center series.

DYNASTIES

The Carey Center is a performance hall like no other, and the Carey family will fight, forgive and find love as they make it the star of the California coast.

Amanda, Serena, Bennett and Justin—don't miss a single Carey family story!

Dear Reader,

Bennett Carey has his hands full in *The Wrong Mr. Right*. When his organized, carefully controlled world is suddenly upended, he needs help. Fast.

Enter Hannah Yates, contractor and pain in Bennett's neck.

Hannah agrees to work for Bennett, mainly because he's willing to pay a substantial bonus if her crew gets the job done on time. That bonus will help grow her company to the next level.

But the two of them quickly discover that working together leads to something neither of them had expected. The question is...what to do about it.

I hope you enjoy the third installment in Dynasties: The Carey Center. Please visit me on Facebook and let me know what you think!

Happy reading!

Until next time,

Maureen

MAUREEN CHILD

THE WRONG MR. RIGHT

HARLEQUIN

DESIRE

DESIRE™

Recycling programs for this product may not exist in your area.

ISBN-13: 978-1-335-73530-0

The Wrong Mr. Right

Copyright © 2021 by Maureen Child

This edition published by arrangement with Harlequin Books S.A.

For questions and comments about the quality of this book, please contact us at CustomerService@Harlequin.com.

Harlequin Enterprises ULC
22 Adelaide St. West, 40th Floor
Toronto, Ontario M5H 4E3, Canada
www.Harlequin.com

Printed in U.S.A.

Maureen Child writes for the Harlequin Desire line and can't imagine a better job. A seven-time finalist for the prestigious Romance Writers of America RITA® Award, Maureen is the author of more than one hundred romance novels. Her books regularly appear on bestseller lists and have won several awards, including a Prism Award, a National Readers' Choice Award, a Colorado Romance Writers Award of Excellence and a Golden Quill Award. She is a native Californian but has recently moved to the mountains of Utah.

Books by Maureen Child

Harlequin Desire

Red Hot Rancher
Jet Set Confessions
Temptation at Christmas
Six Nights of Seduction

Dynasties: The Carey Center

The Ex Upstairs
Ways to Win an Ex
The Wrong Mr. Right

Visit her Author Profile page at Harlequin.com, or maureenchild.com, for more titles.

You can also find Maureen Child on Facebook, along with other Harlequin Desire authors, at Facebook.com/harlequindesireauthors!

To the family and friends who circle the wagons when tragedy strikes. Whoever and wherever you are, know that sometimes a single phone call can help someone hang on.

One

Bennett Carey was a man on the edge.

And his mother was about to push him over.

"Mom," he said, straining for the patience he was not known for, "I don't need you to redecorate my house."

Candace Carey sat opposite his desk and waved one hand at him. The sun caught the huge diamond on her wedding ring and sent flashes of light across his face.

"I'd hardly call it a house, Bennett," she said, and glanced around. "And certainly not a *home*." She shook her head. "Your office here at the company has more personality than that house. You've lived there five years and it still looks as though it's a rental. Or vacant."

Scowling at her, he muttered, "Not nearly vacant enough at the moment."

Ever since his parents had begun what their children were referring to as "the Retirement Wars," there was no telling what Candace would do next. And apparently, Bennett told himself, even in his office at the Carey Corporation headquarters, he wouldn't be safe from his mother's interference. He'd actually offered his assistant, David, a raise— if he could keep Bennett's mother out of his office. David declined.

Bennett couldn't even blame the man. Their father, Martin Carey, had promised his wife that he would retire, take the trips the two of them had always planned to make. But, Bennett told himself, Martin was incapable of walking away from the family corporation. Oh, his dad had meant to retire— he simply couldn't bring himself to turn his back on the family company. Though Bennett was the CEO now, Martin made sure that his son ran *nothing* without his input. So to show her husband how it felt to be deserted in favor of work, Candace had left her husband of nearly forty years and moved in with *Bennett*.

"The walls are beige, Bennett."

"I like beige."

"No one likes beige," his mother countered, lifting her chin, signaling her willingness to do battle. "It's a noncolor. Only slightly better than white." She shivered a little. "You need color in your life, Bennett. In more ways than on the walls of your house. You're in serious danger of becoming just like your father. Before you know it, you'll be devoting your life to this blasted company and letting everything else turn to dust around you."

Standing to face her, he argued that point. "I'm not. I have a life. Hell, I was just up at my cabin in Big Bear."

He'd run there, actually, in an attempt to get away from the family currently driving him nuts. It was supposed to have been a week of peace and quiet. He'd lasted two days. Who the hell could live without the sounds of the city? Without a decent internet connection? Without *concrete?* There was far too much nature at the cabin.

"You haven't had a single woman over in the two weeks I've been living with you."

His jaw dropped and his eyes went wide. "Of course I haven't. You're my *mother.*" When your mom was living in your house, it wasn't exactly conducive to having a one-night stand with a willing female. Hell, unless he could get his mother to move the hell out, he'd probably die a monk.

He couldn't believe they were even having this conversation. Suddenly the damned peace and quiet at the cabin looked more appealing.

"And being your mother," she said, "I'm well aware of how important a good sexual relationship is to a healthy life."

He held up both hands and shook his head. "Stop. I beg you. Just…stop."

She gave an inelegant snort. "I had no idea you were such a prude, Bennett."

"I am not a prude," he ground out, and gave himself a mental pat on the back for not shouting at the woman he'd loved his whole life. "But I'm not discussing sex with my mother."

"Your sisters don't have a problem talking with me about this."

"Yeah," he muttered. "I'm not talking about their sex lives, either." They were his sisters. He didn't want to know.

"Well, I think—"

Bennett's phone rang at just that moment and he could only silently thank whatever gods were taking pity on him. He reached for the desk phone and barked, "Yes?"

As he listened to his assistant, Bennett held up one hand to stop his mother from talking. All he could think was, he'd been grateful to the gods too quickly.

"How bad is it?" he asked.

"Bad enough, sir," David answered. "The fire department's on-site."

"Fine. I'm going there now." He hung up, reached for his suit jacket and swung it on, then buttoned it.

"Sorry Mom, we'll have to continue this discussion later." Or never.

She reacted to his expression and curt tone. "First, tell me what's happened."

"There's been a fire. At The Carey."

She gasped. "Is anyone hurt?"

"I don't know yet." He stalked across the room and tossed back over his shoulder, "I'll let you know when I do."

It took him a little less than a half hour to make the drive from Irvine, California, to Laguna, where their five-star restaurant had stood on the cliff's edge for decades.

The restaurant was a rustic, yet elegant place, built with lots of cedar, weathered from the ocean air and with miles of glass to take advantage of the view. A wide, covered front porch offered navy blue cushioned chairs for waiting crowds. The building itself sat on Pacific Coast Highway, but far enough back from the street that there was room for a dozen stone planters filled with bright splashes of colorful flowers. The parking lot was off to the left and at the back of the restaurant, a wide, slate patio offered seating on the cliffs with an unbeatable view of the Pacific.

At the moment though, there were three fire trucks, a couple of police squad cars and paramedics—which worried Bennet. He hoped to hell all of the employees had gotten out safely. He parked his BMW a block away because of the emergency vehicles and hurried through the mob of people gaping at the huge hole in the restaurant's shake roof and the smoke lifting into the air and twisting in the wind streaming in off the ocean.

Bennett loosened his tie and unbuttoned his shirt collar. He felt like even the air was heavy and sitting in his throat, wrapping itself around the knot already lodged there. There was water everywhere and the stench of burning wood and plastic and God knew what else. Even the ocean wind couldn't dissipate it enough to keep Bennett from tasting it with every breath. *A damn mess*, he thought. And heartbreaking along with it.

"Mr. Carey."

He turned to face a fireman in his late forties. The man's face was soot streaked and his uniform jacket wet with water and chemicals. "One of your employees pointed you out. I'm Captain Hill."

"Is everyone safe?" Bennett's first question. He could think about the rest of this situation once he was assured no one had been hurt.

"Yeah." The man looked toward the restaurant. "Only ones in there at the time were the chefs, and they got out fast. Made the call to us and waited outside."

"That's good." And a huge relief. Buildings could be fixed; lives lost were irreplaceable. "How did it start?"

Captain Hill pulled off his helmet and ran one hand

through his hair. Idly, Bennett wondered how the man's hair was so wet while he was wearing a helmet.

"The inspector will be on-site later today and make the official call. But I can tell you it looked electrical to me. Bad wiring. How old is the building?"

Bennett sighed. "About sixty years." His own fault, Bennett told himself. He should have taken care of this when he became CEO of the company. But with everything else going on, and his father constantly sticking his nose in, who had had the time? He should have made the time. Damn it, being in charge meant making sure *everything* was as it should be.

"Is it all right if I go in? Take a look around?"

Hill frowned a bit, but then said, "It's safe. Dirty and wet, but safe. Just be careful. A few of my men are still inside, so if you need something, ask."

"Right. I will. Thanks." Bennett made his way to the restaurant, stepping over hoses, through puddles and around the firemen currently putting away their equipment.

Once inside, he took a long look around and sighed. It wasn't just the damage from the fire that would have to be dealt with. The efforts to put out that fire had destroyed furniture, walls and floors, as well. This was a nightmare.

"Perfect." He had been in the restaurant just two nights before with Jack Colton, his sister Serena's fiancé. That night, the place had looked as it always had. Elegant, but somehow comfortable at the same time. Pale walls, the color of adobe were adorned with heavy dark beams and wide windows, flanked by brass lamps that looked as if they were made at the turn of the century. Every table was covered with white tablecloths and would normally boast brass vases holding seasonal flowers. The silverware was heavy, the crystal was hand carved, the service was impeccable and the food was unmatched anywhere.

Now, he thought, it looked as though a war had been fought in the middle of the dining room. And, he supposed it had. The war had been won, thank God, but there was another battle yet to come. The traditions in this place tugged at him even as he realized that it would all change now.

And it seemed that lately, he was surrounded by change. His sisters shifting things around. His brother, Justin, making himself scarce—avoiding the family. His mother, for God's sake, moving in with him. And his father refusing to let go and making Bennett's life far more complicated than it had to be.

Looking at The Carey, he accepted the damage as he would one more boulder dropped onto his shoulders.

He stepped past the sinuous, winding bar toward the swinging door into the kitchen and couldn't swallow another sigh. "Yeah, we won't be serving dinner anytime soon." Which posed a problem well beyond the mess he was staring at.

Now that he knew his employees were safe, Bennett could focus on the issue that was staring him in the face. He had a formal dinner planned here at the restaurant in four weeks. Invitations had gone out. Media announcements had been made. It was too late to change the venue and damned if he'd cancel it. So that left him one choice only.

Taking out his cell phone, Bennett hit the speed dial and waited until his assistant answered. "David. Get the best contractor in the county on the phone. I need them working on the restaurant ASAP."

"Yes, sir."

Bennett hung up a moment later and continued toward the kitchen, kicking trash out of his way as he went. The whole place was a wreck, he thought, gaze scanning the damage done by the men and women who had saved the building. It wasn't just the kitchen that would need to be restored.

The floor—hundred-year-old oak planks—would have to be sanded and refinished. The bar was smoke stained as well as waterlogged, and the bar mirror had been shattered along with most of the liquor bottles. The heavy walnut tables had been tipped over and just a cursory glance showed him that some of them needed repairs, too. Not to mention the chairs.

He opened the notepad on his phone and started a list. From flooring to liquor to walls and furniture, Bennett muttered curses under his breath with every addition. Still, making that list gave him something to focus on. Lists, if used properly, he thought, could solve any problem. They were the way Bennett kept his world from spinning out of control.

He pushed through the swinging door and his first glance at the kitchen made him groan aloud. "Four weeks. Four lousy weeks until this has to be a working, top-grade kitchen."

"Yeah, I don't see that happening."

Bennett looked left and watched his head chef, John Henry Mitchell walk toward him. African American, he was six foot five, with short, black curly hair and sharp brown eyes. He was built like an NFL lineman and was a damn artist in a kitchen.

"John Henry." Bennett held out his hand and the other man shook it. "Relieved you made it out safely."

"So am I." The big man's voice rolled around the room with the sonorous roar of thunder. "I had two of the sous-chefs in here, prepping for tonight."

"They're okay?" Bennett asked, even though he'd already been assured that everyone had made it out.

"They're a little rattled, but they'll do." John Henry shook his head and stared at the far wall. "It started there," he said, pointing at a section of burned-out wall. "I didn't notice right away. Probably would have if I hadn't been in the refrigerator, going over supplies."

"Not your fault."

"Oh, I know that," he said, turning to look at Bennett again. "It was the wiring, Bennett. Firemen said it just erupted and from there, spread like hellfire.

Ran right up the wall and across the ceiling." His gaze followed his words and so did Bennett's. "From there, it went into the attic and the roof. This old cedar and the shake roof…just fed the flames and, well, you know the rest." He shrugged massive shoulders. "I got the boys out of here, called the fire department, then stood outside and watched."

"Yeah." Bennett kicked a piece of charred wood and listened to it skitter across the floor. The stainless steel prep counters were filthy and pooled with dirty water. "Thanks for getting that call in so quickly."

"This is a hell of a thing, Bennett."

"It damn sure is."

A couple of minutes of silence stretched out as both men surveyed the damage. "What're you going to do about the formal dinner? It's just four weeks out."

"I know," Bennett muttered. "I've got my assistant calling a contractor now."

John Henry laughed and it sounded like a landslide. "It's coming onto summer, Bennett. Every contractor in Orange County is going to be busy— putting in pools and patios and God knows what else. I've got my own guy starting a retaining wall in my backyard on Monday."

"I'll find one," he said, and it sounded like a vow even to himself. "If I have to offer bonuses or double pay, I'll do it."

"Well, that should take care of it," John Henry mused.

"You bet it will," Bennett said, shooting his friend a hard look. "Money motivates better than anything I know. I'll get the damn contractor. The dinner's still on, John Henry. You keep refining the menu. Steaks of course—"

"Of course."

The Carey restaurant offered the best steaks in California, hands down. And that was *one* tradition that wasn't about to change.

"You handle the rest of the menu," Bennett said, waving one hand.

John Henry laughed a little. "Yeah, I figured to do that. I would never leave that up to you."

Wryly, Bennet smiled. "Good call." He took a deep breath and scowled at the stench of smoke and burned wood. Then he looked around the destruction again before fixing his gaze on his old friend. "So do you need anything?"

"No. I'm good."

"We'll pay salaries whether the crew is working or not until the restaurant's up and running again."

John Henry gave him a small smile. "I already told everyone you would."

Bennett's eyebrows lifted. "That sure of yourself?"

"That sure of you, Bennett." He pushed both hands into the pockets of his khaki slacks. "I've never known you to *not* care about your employees."

Embarrassed, uncomfortable, Bennett brushed that aside. It wasn't like he deserved a reward or something. It was just the right thing to do. Still, he made a mental note to begin a new list with everything their employees might need to hold on until the restaurant reopened. "No reason for you to stick around, John Henry. Go on home. I'll let you know when the work starts here."

"Good," the other man said, "I've got a few ideas for some improvements."

"I'll bet you do," Bennett mused.

Laughing again, John Henry said, "Hey, as long as we're rebuilding, we might as well make those changes I've been ragging you about for the last five years. For example, higher counters so a man doesn't have to bend in half to work…"

"Fine. Make a list."

John Henry laughed again and slapped Bennett on the back. "How many lists have you started already today?"

"Two," he admitted with a shake of his head. "And more to come no doubt."

Bennett knew he was going to give John Henry whatever the hell he wanted as far as the kitchen went. The man was the best damn chef in California. Keeping him happy meant no other restaurant would be able to steal him away. "When I talk plans with the contractor, you'll be in on it."

John Henry nodded, and when the old friends looked at each other, they both laughed.

Bennett sighed and said, smiling, "Yeah, you

knew you'd be in on that conversation. Have your list ready, and I'll let you know as soon as I find the contractor."

John Henry grinned. "Better get on that. Four weeks is not a lot of time."

A few days later, Bennett was at the end of his patience. That cliff he'd been clinging to a few days ago suddenly looked comfortable compared to where he was at the moment. He hated to admit it, but John Henry had been right.

Bennett's assistant had called every well-known contractor in Orange County and from each one had gotten a resounding no. Hell, Bennett had even asked a few friends to call in favors and nothing had worked. Not even the promise of a boatload of money. What was the world coming to when *money* didn't solve problems?

Every big outfit was busy as hell, thanks to summer looming ever closer. And Bennett was in a serious bind. His restaurant had to be restored, and the only way that would happen is if he took a chance on a small company with several good online reviews.

Which was why he was here, at The Carey, meeting with a woman who didn't look big enough to swing a hammer. He watched that woman now as she moved through the restaurant, checking out the damage. She was tiny. Just a little over five feet, but she was impressive.

She had a small, compact body with curves he shouldn't be noticing. Her hair was short, too, with black spikes and curls framing a face that was heart shaped, with a full mouth, high cheekbones and green eyes that were bright and shining with eagerness. She wasn't at all what he'd been expecting.

Hannah Yates of Yates Construction.

His gaze locked onto her as she moved around the room, and he scowled a little as he realized that he was having to fight to concentrate on the situation. Hannah Yates was too distracting—which he did not need at the moment. What he needed was a damn good contractor. Instead, he was watching a sexy pixie.

According to her, it had been her father Harry's company until she took it over three years before. She'd shown up with references, pictures of the other jobs she'd completed, both before and after, and she hadn't stopped talking since she'd walked in the door. Even now, she was talking to herself as she roamed the wreckage, shaking her head.

From what he could tell, she seemed to know her business. He just wasn't sure a small company would be enough to get the job done in the time he required.

She was busily making notes on the tablet she carried, and occasionally, she took out a measuring tape and ran it across a burned-out surface. It wasn't easy for Bennett, but he kept quiet and let her concentrate. She reached across the bar with that measuring tape and he absolutely did not notice how her jeans cupped her butt. Hannah Yates was his last hope of getting the restaurant back up and running in time.

"How soon do you need this done?" she asked, tossing him a glance over her shoulder.

"Four weeks."

"Hah!" She grinned, shook her head as if she were talking to a nutcase and went back to muttering to herself.

Shrugging out of her dark green hoodie stamped with Yates Construction across the back, she tossed it onto an overturned table leg. Then she shook her head and pushed one small hand through that short, black hair. Something stirred inside him and he fought it down.

He was out of options. Bennett had tried everything. This woman and her small company were his only hope. It wouldn't be easy to trust her with this job, but he didn't have much choice here, either. And that was hard to take for a man used to being in charge. It was a hell of a thing, he thought, to be forced to put his trust in a woman who looked like a sexy elf.

Two

Four weeks. Hannah Yates smothered another laugh and told herself he'd been kidding.

His gaze followed her as she moved through what had once been the most exclusive restaurant in Laguna. God knew she wasn't a stranger to scenes like this, but she could at least take a second to think it was a shame. Heck, she'd never had the chance to eat here—who could afford it? And now she was finally inside, seeing it at its absolute worst.

She had the distinct feeling she was seeing Bennett Carey at his worst, too. He didn't look happy to be dealing with her, but if he wanted to save his restaurant, he'd have to get over that.

Just look at him, she thought. Standing amid the rubble, looking like a model for *GQ* or something. Somehow, he'd even managed to keep the shine on his Italian shoes in spite of the rubble and grime around them. When she turned to check another measurement, Hannah actually *felt* him watching her.

She knew he was actively wondering if she could do the job he needed. Because she was short and cute, men tended to underestimate her. Well, it wasn't the first time she'd had to prove herself. She could do it again.

Just because he was, without a doubt, the most gorgeous man she'd ever seen, didn't mean she could take her eyes off the *real* prize.

Which was the possibility of landing this job.

She wasn't looking for a man, and if she were, she wouldn't be looking at Bennett Carey. He was way out of her league, and she knew it. Didn't hurt to look, she supposed, but *touching* was definitely off the table. Hell, she'd been burned before by dating a wealthy man and had no intention of ever making that mistake again.

But working for him, that was something else.

She picked her way through the detritus left behind by the fire and the men and women who'd put out the flames. The oak floors were scarred and even scorched in a few places. They'd need to be sanded, repaired and stained again. Tables needed to be reinforced, and that gorgeous bar needed exactly what the floors did.

No, she'd never been here before, so she only had hearsay to know it had been a showplace. All she had to do now was convince Bennett Carey that she and her crew could make it a showplace again.

This restaurant was a landmark in Laguna, and if she were the one to bring it back to life… That would put her company on the map. So to speak.

For a moment, Hannah let her mind wander to just how much The Carey project could impact her future. Her dad, Harry, had built a small, but honest company with a good reputation. When she took over from him three years before, she'd built on what he'd given her, and already, their reputation was growing, spreading—which was the only reason Bennett Carey was interviewing her in the first place. Well, that, and he didn't have a lot of choices right now.

She knew as well as he did that every big company in the county was already booked for summer jobs that were starting now. So his choices were few and that gave *her* the upper hand here. He needed her and Yates Construction.

Even more than she needed this job.

All she had to do was play the situation well.

Finishing up her notes, Hannah walked to where Bennett Carey waited and stopped right in front of him. "You've got some serious damage here."

"Yes," he said wryly, "I'm aware."

Ignoring that, she glanced at her tablet, scrolled through the notes, then looked up at him. "All I'm saying is, it's a big job."

"Are you incapable of handling it?"

"Hardly." Hannah tapped one finger at the logo on the left breast of her red T-shirt. "This says Yates Construction. That means I construct."

He took a breath and released it on a sigh. "My question was more in the line of wondering if your company was big enough to handle the job."

She stiffened, lifted her chin and straightened up to her full five-foot-four height. "My company can handle *any* job. I gave you references. Call any of them you like."

"I talked to a couple of them while you were making notes."

"Well, you don't waste any time, do you?"

"There's no time to waste," he pointed out. "And I checked you out before I set up this meeting. You get excellent reviews, but none of your jobs have been this size."

True. Yates Construction had a good reputation, but most of the jobs they did were residential or small businesses. She was proud of every one of them. But The Carey restaurant was something else. Something *more.* Which was why she wanted this job so badly. Working for the Carey family would give her entry into the world of big money and bored people looking for a way to spend it.

"If you put them all together they are."

"My point is—"

"I know what your point is," Hannah interrupted. "My crew can do it."

He didn't look convinced, she thought, but he hadn't said no, either. And men like him—wealthy, powerful—never had a problem saying no, which told her just how much he needed her company. He didn't look happy about that, either. Honestly, with his stern features and dark blue eyes, he looked like the world's most gorgeous statue. And she half wondered if he looked as good naked as he did in that impeccable suit he was wearing.

Beside the point, Hannah.

Refocusing, she said, "I've got more *before* and *after* pictures of our completed jobs here on my tablet if you want to see them."

She called them up and Bennett quietly swiped through them. Hannah knew the pictures were impressive because she'd taken them. She'd been onsite for every one of those jobs and knew just how good her crew was. His scowl deepened as if he really hated having to admit she was as good as she claimed to be.

A minute or so later, he handed the tablet back to her.

"I'll need the work completed in four weeks," he said again.

Hannah looked up at Bennett Carey and exploded

in laughter. He hadn't been kidding. Honestly, she should have tried to hold it in, because she really wanted this job. But on the other hand, the man was standing in a fire-ravaged restaurant wearing a suit that probably cost more than her truck and issuing ridiculous orders like a king.

"Something funny?" He gave her a look meant to intimidate.

It didn't.

"Oh yes, that was very funny. Seriously, I thought you were kidding when you said that before. Four weeks. To fix all of *this*?" She held up one hand and told herself to get a grip. She was a professional, after all. "Sorry. I probably shouldn't have laughed, but honestly, look around, Mr. Carey. Four weeks?"

He did give the destruction another long look before shifting his gaze back to her. "I've got a very important formal dinner scheduled to be held here in four weeks. There's no postponing. There's no moving it to another venue. I want it here."

"And I want to be five foot ten," she muttered. One of his eyebrows arched, but she continued. "I understand, but you must know that it's practically impossible for anyone to get this job done in the time required."

"So I've been told," he said through gritted teeth. "Repeatedly."

"And yet here we are." He frowned, and she wondered if that was a permanent expression.

"Impossible or not, I need this done."

"Does anyone ever actually get away with saying no to you?"

His lips twitched briefly, and she thought he might be even more gorgeous with a real smile. Though she doubted she'd see one.

"I don't like the word *no*," he admitted.

"Huh. Neither do I. So we have that in common." He didn't speak, but she didn't need him to. Probably better if he didn't. He was clearly used to giving orders, and she was never very good at taking them. Hannah took another look around the inside of the restaurant and did some mental calculations.

If she said no, he'd only try someone else. If she said yes, it could either be the best thing she'd ever done or an exercise in futility. But oh, she wanted to say yes.

Hannah took a breath. Every one of the bigger, more well-known companies he'd undoubtedly spoken to had told him not only that they were already booked, but that expecting the job to be done so quickly was ridiculous. Well, she was hardly the biggest contractor in Orange County. But even if she said so herself, she was the best.

"Okay, so other contractors have told you the same thing."

"Yes." He ground out that single word. "Along with the fact that they're completely booked for the next two months."

"So, you really need me and my crew," she said. She

wasn't his first choice but if she pulled this off, she'd be everyone else's first choice from there on out. Yates Construction was a damn good firm and once she'd proven that fact to Bennett Carey, they'd be on their way.

"Basically," he said.

"We can do it, but I can't promise you four weeks," she said, meeting his gaze squarely.

"If you can't deliver in four weeks, I can't use you."

"I'm all you've got," she pointed out. Well, judging by his expression, King Carey didn't like hearing *that*. Whether he liked it or not though, they both knew it was true. Without Yates Construction, he was simply out of luck.

He looked around again, as if reminding himself just how bad the situation was. Then he looked back at her. "How long would you need?"

Now it was her turn to meet his gaze. She didn't need to look around the room again; she'd seen all she needed to. "In a perfect world, eight weeks."

"Last time I checked, the world is far from perfect," he pointed out.

"True. So, say six weeks." He didn't look happy, but then he probably never did. Still, she wanted this job. "If I did it in four weeks, I'd have to pay overtime to my crew every day. We'd be putting in a lot of late hours."

"So it is possible."

She grinned. He might be grumpy but he was quick. "Figured you'd pick up on that. Sure, it's possible, if you don't mind working your crew…and yourself, to death."

"Four weeks of overtime doesn't sound so bad."

"Not bad," she agreed, nodding. "But expensive. It would significantly impact my estimate on the repairs."

"I'm not worried about that."

Good to know. Another reminder of just how different they were, she decided. Hannah couldn't imagine not worrying about what something cost.

He scrubbed one hand across the back of his neck and Hannah could almost feel tension vibrating off the man. It took a long minute or two, but finally, he said, "I'll handle the overtime for your crew."

"Yeah," she said with a short laugh. "I know."

He glanced around the room, then met her gaze again. "What you don't know is, if you finish the job in four weeks there's a bonus in it for you, as well."

Everything inside her went on alert, but she didn't show it. There was never any telling what an über-rich person might do. His idea of bonus and hers might be light-years apart anyway. Probably were. Still, she had to ask. "What kind of bonus?"

He scowled, and she knew he wasn't happy about the situation.

"Fifty thousand. Over the cost of the job itself."

Hannah's jaw wanted to drop but she managed to regain control before she let him see what that offer meant to her. Silently, she gave herself a mental pat on the back for keeping her excitement from him.

Wouldn't do to let him see just how badly she wanted this job and that bonus.

Still, her heartbeat galloped, and Hannah could have sworn she saw stars. *Fifty thousand dollars* as a bonus? Over and above what she would have charged him for the job—including overtime—anyway? In a split second, she saw what that kind of money could do for her and the company.

She could pay off loans on new equipment, settle every bill hanging over her head and she could give her crew the kind of bonus that they all deserved. While she was thinking, relishing the kind of monumental change that amount of money could make, Bennett spoke again.

Apparently, he thought she was going to refuse him, because he blurted, "Fine. A hundred thousand."

She nearly staggered and, this time, didn't bother to hide her shock. "Are you out of your mind?"

One of his eyebrows winged up. "You're not interested?"

"Well, of course I'm interested," Hannah snapped, forgetting all about her silent vow to be polite to the man. "I'm not an idiot."

"So it's something else," he said. "Do you need more as an incentive?"

"No," she countered, though she was tempted to see just how high he would go. "But I think you need a therapist."

He choked out what might have been a strangled

laugh. It was hard to tell, but then, he didn't look like the kind of man who did a lot of laughing. He was probably just out of practice.

"Is it a deal or not?"

She didn't answer that right away. She had to do some fast thinking, figuring, mentally shifting her crew around from other jobs to accommodate this one. And even while she did it, she knew she would take the job. She needed it. Not just for the ridiculous bonus but because the cachet of working on The Carey would be a jumping-off point into all sorts of first-class renovations, restorations… Seriously, the mind boggled at the opportunity that would be just waiting for her to grab it.

Yet again, she didn't want him to know how eager she really was for this job. The only reason he was talking to her at all was that all of the bigger companies were booked. So let him wonder if she was going to turn him down, as well. Besides, it was going to take a second or two for her to find her voice again.

A hundred-thousand-dollar bonus. Yeah, she needed a second.

"Four weeks," she muttered, taking another look around.

"Not a day more," he told her.

"We'll be pulling a lot of late nights to get it done in time."

"Already agreed to the overtime," he said simply.

"Yeah, you did." Imagine having a client *not* bitch about paying overtime.

"Then there's the bonus," he added, like an adult holding out a candy bar to a sulky child.

She looked up at him. He was really tall. His dark blond hair was just a little rumpled, and she thought that he'd probably been running his hands through it. And oddly enough, she liked knowing that nerves and worry could affect him, too. His eyes were the same shade as a sapphire and glittered just as brightly. She really was thinking way too much about how gorgeous he was, but honestly, she'd have had to be blind not to notice.

"A hundred thousand dollars," she repeated. Nope, didn't get any easier to say—much less believe.

"That's what I said."

Clearly the rich were *really* different. How desperate was he, to toss that much money around? Bad for him, potentially good for her. He didn't seem dangerous, and it was his money, after all. She already knew rich people were eccentric. Of course poor people were just called crazy, but that had nothing to do with anything.

Narrowing her gaze on him, she said, "This dinner must be really important to you."

"It is."

"I'll have to shuffle some of my current jobs around to make this work."

"You'll be rewarded," he reminded her.

"There is that," she mused, still trying to keep from letting him see what this meant to her.

"So," he said impatiently, "is it a deal or not?"

She held out one hand. "It's a deal."

His big hand completely enveloped hers, and the heat his touch engendered swept through her entire body. There was a sizzle in her blood, and just for a second, her mind actually blurred. And Hannah had to wonder if, bonus or not, she'd made a mistake in dealing with Bennett Carey.

To settle herself, she pulled her hand free of his grip and started talking again.

"You're sure you're okay with the overtime," she said, gauging his reaction. "My crew will be putting in a lot of extra hours."

His jaw tightened briefly, but he gave her a sharp nod. "I told you I'm fine with it. As long as my schedule isn't interrupted, we have a deal."

Shaking her head a little, Hannah muttered under her breath.

"What was that?"

She really needed to just *think* these things. "I said, maybe you should be interrupted more often. You seem wound a little tight."

"Thank you for your observation," he said stiffly. "I'll keep it in mind." He checked what looked like a solid gold watch. "When you begin work, my head chef, John Henry Mitchell, will be contacting you on some specific changes he wants to the kitchen."

He'd surprised her again. He didn't seem like the kind of man to release even a tiny bit of power to someone else. "Wow. You're giving over decisions to your chef?"

"I don't cook."

"Yeah. I guessed that." He probably had a personal chef at home, too. "I'll need the key."

"Yeah. I guessed that." Her lips twitched when he threw her words back at her.

He handed the key over. Hannah's fist curled around it, and she held on tightly to her future.

With one last glance around at the rubble that had once been a kitchen, he said, "I'll leave you to get started."

When he walked out of the restaurant, Hannah had the distinct feeling she should have saluted.

At the family meeting that afternoon, Bennett sat back quietly, observing the Careys—siblings and parents—and only half listened to the conversations flying around the room. Idly, his gaze shifted to the floor-to-ceiling windows. Tinted to keep the sunlight quietly at bay, they still provided a view of a deep blue sky and several other chrome-and-glass buildings clustered together in the office park.

There was a blue smudge in the distance that was the ocean, and closer, was the constant traffic on the 405 freeway. Here, high above the city and the noise, the silence could be deafening—unless you were in a

Carey family meeting. Maybe, he told himself, that was why their youngest brother, Justin, managed to avoid these meetings regularly.

Another irritation for Bennett. He didn't know what Justin was up to, and he didn't like being in the dark. One day soon, he and his little brother were going to have a long talk.

During a pause in the incessant chatter, Bennett caught everyone's attention by announcing, "I've hired a contractor to make the repairs on The Carey."

Instantly of course, the questions started flying.

"Who?" his sister Amanda asked.

"Hannah Yates of Yates Construction," he answered.

"A woman," Serena said, smiling and nodding. "Good for you, Bennett."

"I didn't hire her because she was a woman."

"You probably didn't notice," Amanda muttered. Serena snorted.

Bennett frowned, because whether his sisters would believe it or not, he'd noticed *everything* about Hannah Yates. From those amazing green eyes, to the curves packed neatly into such a tiny frame and the way she moved, all grace and confidence.

"Yates Construction?" His father, Martin, wrinkled his brow. "Never heard of them."

"And you know all of the construction companies in Orange County, do you?" His mother Candace's voice was so sweet it could have caused cavities, but the sting was still there.

"No," Martin said, "but I—"

"I'm sure Bennett's taken care of checking credentials and references."

"Thanks, Mom," he said tightly. He half expected her to give him a smiley face sticker. "Yes, I did."

He glanced at the dim sunlight pouring through the windows again. He knew that outside, there was a lush greenbelt that lay like a ribbon uncoiled to fall where it may. And right at the moment, Bennett wished he were there. In the quiet.

"How long has this Hannah Yates been doing construction work?" Amanda asked.

Bennett looked at her. "Apparently all her life, but she took over her father's company three years ago." He managed to slide a quick look his father's way. After all, Bennett had taken over the Carey Company and yet, Martin Carey refused to hand over the reins entirely. Seemed to him that Martin could learn a thing or two from Hannah's father.

"Can't be easy for her," Amanda said, "running her own company in that field."

"Mandy's right." Serena spoke up and fiddled with her brand-new emerald engagement ring while she did. "She must be good at what she does. I imagine she faces all sorts of problems while trying to build a company in what is generally considered a man's territory."

"Yeah," Bennett grumbled. "I'm not looking to lead the feminist charge. I just need a contractor and Hannah Yates says she can do it."

"And you're taking her word for it?" His father again, and Bennett bit his tongue to keep from saying what he'd like to say.

Martin was supposed to have retired months ago. But the old man was clinging to the Carey Corporation as he would to a slippery edge on the side of a mountain. His fingers couldn't be pried off. While he could understand his father's reluctance to let go, Bennett had trained for this job his whole life. He was capable and eager to take over the reins of the family legacy.

Bennett was the CEO but Martin made sure he kept his hand in well… Everything.

"Believe it or not, Dad, I researched her. She has a good reputation and her former clients can't say enough positive things about her."

"And that's good enough for you?"

Patience, he reminded himself. Bennett loved his family, and it was only that love that helped him hold on to what little patience he had. God knew it wasn't his strong suit. He'd always believed in charging ahead, going after what you wanted, letting no one and nothing slow you down. So holding back for his father's sake was costing him.

"Like Mom said, like I just told you, I checked her out. And it's not like we've got a lot of options, Dad." He shrugged and shook his head. "Every one of the big, well-known contractors around is already booked for the summer."

"So we're settling," Martin said, with a huff of disapproval.

Bennett looked at his sisters for support. Serena winced. Amanda hid a smile behind her hand. No help there.

"If you had retired as you were supposed to," Candace said, capturing the attention of everyone in the room, "we'd be on a Caribbean cruise right now and you wouldn't know anything about this."

Martin scowled. "But I do know."

"Yes, exactly. You do. Why? Because you won't leave this company as you promised you would," Candace said, and turned away from him.

"Aw, Candy…"

Bennett rubbed the bridge of his nose. The Retirement Wars continued. Seriously, between his parents, the company, the fire at The Carey and his missing brother, Bennett felt the ledge under his feet crumbling. And that didn't even take into account his sisters, their new fiancés and their ability to poke at him.

"The pictures of her work are really amazing," Amanda tossed in, and Bennet wanted to kiss his sister for the surprising show of support.

"It is," Serena tossed in as she took the tablet from Amanda. "I especially love the renovations done to the kitchens. Since that's exactly what we need done, I think that's a good sign."

"Someone's kitchen in their house is a whole different thing from a professional kitchen in a damn near legendary restaurant," Martin grumbled. No one commented.

"She can have it done in time for the party?" Candace asked, still ignoring her husband.

"It'll cost overtime, but yes." Bennett kept talking to avoid hearing his father's opinion.

"You're paying overtime?"

Apparently, he couldn't avoid his father's opinion. The old man's face was florid, and Bennett could practically see his blood pressure rise. Probably wouldn't be a good idea to mention a one-hundred-thousand-dollar bonus.

Looking into his father's eyes, Bennett said, "I'm paying whatever I have to, to get the job done."

"As a CEO should," Candace said with a knowing glare at her husband.

"Fine." Martin sat back, glowering at his son. "I just hope you know what you're doing."

Bennett remembered the heat he'd felt when he'd shaken Hannah Yates's hand. That fast, electrical jolt of something… Interesting. Something he hadn't expected and didn't have time for.

As he thought back to the sexy pixie laughing up at him, Bennett heard himself say, "Yeah. So do I."

Three

At her father's house a couple hours later, Hannah sat on a dining room chair with her head between her knees, breathing deeply. Her head still felt a little light and her mind was spinning with possibilities.

Absently, she stared down at the wide oak floorboards and focused on a single knot in the wood that looked like a wide eye staring back at her. Her heart was racing, her mouth was dry and she was pretty sure her right eye was twitching.

"You okay, peach?" Her father's voice as he patted her back hard enough to dislodge whatever he thought might be stuck in her throat.

"Ow, Dad," she said, "I'm not choking. I'm okay. Really. I think."

"All right, then." Hank stepped around in front of her. Hannah could see the scarred toes of his work boots. "If you're okay, you want to say all of that again?"

She mumbled while still trying to take deep, even breaths.

"For God's sake, girl, sit up and say that again. *Slowly.*"

When Hannah was sure she wouldn't pass out or start hyperventilating, she sat up, planted her hands on her knees and looked up at her dad. "Bennett Carey's paying all overtime with no bitching—well almost none. *And* he's giving us a one-hundred-*thousand*-dollar bonus if we complete the repairs on time."

Now it was Hank's turn to look a little pale. He reached out one hand until he found the back of the chair next to his daughter and then dropped into it. He frowned, scrubbed one hand across his gray grizzled jaw, swallowed hard, then asked, "Is he sane?"

She choked out a laugh. Funny that Hank had said what she'd been wondering.

"I don't know. I don't think so." She thought back on their conversation and could only come up with, "At least, he didn't seem dangerous. I just think he needs this job done fast. And he doesn't seem like the kind of man who's used to having people say no to him."

"More than one kind of danger," Hank muttered.

True. She remembered Bennett Carey and his eyes and his mouth when he talked or scowled or both and the buzz of something interesting that had happened the moment she'd shaken his hand. And yes, there was more than one kind of danger. But for this chance, this opportunity, she was willing to risk it.

"Dad." Her gaze locked onto his as she spelled out her motivation one word at a time. "I'm not interested in that kind of danger. Already been burned, remember?"

"Oh, I remember," Hank told her, his gaze searching hers. "I want to make sure you do."

"Hard to forget." She'd dated a rich client once. He'd been smooth and slick and had sent her flowers for no reason at all. He'd swept her off her feet and into an engagement that had nearly cost her everything. She'd trusted too easily, believed too deeply and eventually fell way too far. She wouldn't be making the mistake of falling for another rich guy, no matter how tempting he was.

"I just don't want to see you get tangled up in something hard again, Hannah."

"I'm not tangled," she argued, refusing to remember that buzz of interest. "I'm taking a job. For the money. For the bonus. Dad," she said softly. "One. Hundred. Thousand. Dollars."

He still looked concerned. "To get an eight-week job done in four weeks."

"Well yeah," Hannah muttered with a shrug. "There's that."

And truth be told, she was a little worried about it,

hence the hyperventilating. Yes, she'd assured King Carey that her crew could do it, but she knew it wasn't going to be easy. Still, with carte blanche for overtime and that amazing bonus—maybe King Carey really was crazy—she would find a way to pull it off.

Hank Yates propped one elbow on the dining table that had been sitting in the same spot in the same house for the last thirty years. It was maple, and looked as if it had been through a war and come out the victor. A little battered, a little scarred, but through it all, still polished once a week and still standing.

And that, Hannah thought, was something you could say about the whole house. A quick look around at the rose-colored walls with the cream crown molding; the gleaming, if scarred oak floors; the burgundy couch and chairs; and the black recliner that was Hank's personal heaven.

And Hank himself, for that matter. She looked at her father and saw the man who had been her hero and role model all of her life.

Hank was five foot eight and still muscular from his years of working construction. His face was weathered from spending his life in the sun, but the wrinkles around his eyes and mouth were from smiling. Not much got her father down, and she knew that he had a spine of steel.

Hank's wife, Hannah's mother, had walked out on the family when Hannah was only three. The woman had decided that being a wife and mother was stifling her need for happiness. So she walked out, divorced Hank a year later, and she'd never been seen again.

That was fine with Hannah. Sure, when she was twelve or thirteen, she'd wanted a mom to talk to about periods and boys and everything else a growing girl needed to know. Her friend's mother had helped her through a few questions, and she was still grateful for it. But Hank had stepped in, too. If he'd been embarrassed, Hannah hadn't seen it.

He was just there. A rock. As he'd always been. He was the one stable point in Hannah's universe. Always there. Always steady. Always ready to stand behind her when she needed him. He'd been both mother and father to Hannah all her life and she couldn't love him more.

Hank had raised her on construction sites and his crew had been her very protective uncles. They'd taught her carpentry, plumbing, roofing, electrical— everything she might need to run her own crew. As she was now, and had been since taking over Yates Construction. Some of the guys were still working with her, and even Hank got tired of fishing every day and would show up at a job just to keep his hand in.

She'd need him to give a hand on this job.

"Have you talked to Steve?" Hank finally asked.

Her foreman. "No. I wanted to tell you first. Ask you what you thought about it."

He laughed shortly. "You're asking me *after* you made the decision."

True. "Well…okay, yes."

"Like when you bought that old truck, drove it home and the engine fell out on the driveway?" He smiled as he said it, and Hannah laughed.

"I was seventeen," she reminded him, and didn't bother to point out that once she and her dad had worked on that truck, she drove it for five years.

"Doesn't seem much has changed," Hank mused.

"I suppose not," she agreed. "But Dad, how could I turn that down? Once we complete the job, we can pay off the last of that loan and still have enough left over to buy new equipment and—"

Hank held up one hand and shook his head. "I get it. I do. And I want what you want."

"Thanks, Dad—"

"*But*," he added with a smile, "that said, I don't want you working yourself to death just for a bonus. Just to get rid of that loan."

Hannah leaned forward and laid one hand on Hank's arm. "It's not just that. Paying off past mistakes, Dad. We get this done for King Carey—"

He snorted. *"King Carey?"*

She shrugged as she remembered that aloof look on Bennett Carey's features and how he'd given the impression that he was expecting her to genuflect. Not to mention his impatience, the take-charge attitude and the nearly imperious attitude.

"That's what I was calling him in my mind," she admitted. "He's bossy. Sort of…aristocratic, I guess. Anyway. If we get this job done for the Carey family—" she paused, took a breath and sighed at the possibilities "—we'd have them on our résumé. We'd get the bigger jobs in the county. We could take Yates Construction right to the top."

He watched her for a long minute. "But no pressure?"

She laughed, gave his arm a squeeze. "Exactly. I'm going to call Steve in a minute and tell him to get the crew together." She sat back and started thinking. She'd been over every inch of the destruction in The Carey, but she needed to walk it again, now that she had the go-ahead to work the project.

"It's an old building," she mused aloud, "and we know, because of the fire, the wiring was a problem in the kitchen." Tapping one finger against her chin. "We'll have Marco Benzi come in and check the rest of the wiring in the building."

Marco was the best electrician she knew. He and his guys could cut into the walls in select spots to make sure the wiring in the rest of the building wouldn't be an issue.

"Good plan."

She grinned. "The ceiling's got to come down and the damage in the attic fixed. The roof's in pretty good shape—except for the burned-out portion—"

"Naturally."

Another fast grin. "Tiny and Carol can take care of ripping out the ruined roof beams and shingles while the rest of us do the demo on the kitchen. Most of the counters have got to go, so we'll pull all of them and rebuild uniformly. Some of the white oak floorboards are scarred up and a couple are charred where burning pieces of the ceiling dropped onto them. We'll have to sand and refinish and to make sure it matches the rest of the room, we'll just sand down the whole kitchen."

"Makes sense. Devin Colier is the man there."

"True." She paused and looked around. "I should have my tablet. Or paper. Write all this down."

Hank laughed shortly. "You'll remember. Always did have a sharp mind."

"You're my favorite human," Hannah said, grinning. "You're right. I'll remember." She always used Devin when she needed floors repaired or refinished. The man was a genius, and when he retired, she was going to be heartbroken.

In four weeks, Hannah would be able to prove to Bennett Carey just how good she was at her job.

"And," she said with a wince, "I'm going to need you, Dad. I know you've got that fishing trip planned with Tom Jetter, but—"

He waved that off. "It'll wait. Tom and I can both come in and help."

Tom had worked for Yates Construction for thirty years, so having him on board for this job would be a huge help, too.

"That'd be great."

Hank gave her a pat, stood up and walked to the kitchen. She followed and gave a quick look around.

Sage green walls, forest green cabinets and white quartz countertops. She and her father had redone the kitchen just two years before, and she still loved it.

The old Craftsman-style house in Long Beach, California, had been Hannah's classroom. Over the years, her father had taught her plumbing, carpentry, masonry—when they laid the stone patio in the backyard—and every other thing a contractor needed to know.

She'd built a four-poster bed for herself at sixteen and at seventeen had renovated an old closet into a half bath powder room.

Hannah knew every square inch of this house and though she lived in her own place now, this would always be home.

Hank poured some coffee and she automatically asked, "How many cups have you had?"

He rolled his eyes and took a deliberate, satisfying sip. "Who's the parent here?"

Her eyebrows arched. "Sometimes I wonder."

"You're a funny girl." Hank sat at the kitchen table and pushed out another chair with a shove of his foot. "Call Steve, let him know what's going on, then we'll make your list and start lining up supplies."

"Okay," she agreed, and dropped onto the chair. As she hit speed dial for her foreman, she gave her father a long look. "But I'm keeping an eye on you. The doctor said no more than three cups of coffee a day."

Hank snorted. "What does he know?"

Hannah sighed and waited for Steve to pick up. Her father's ulcer worried her, but if she could get him to give up his two pots of coffee a day, that would help.

Beyond the everyday worries was Bennett Carey. She couldn't share this with her dad, of course. He would instantly be concerned about her making the same mistake all over again, which she wouldn't. She wasn't looking to date Bennett Carey—although, as she thought of him again—with his piercing blue eyes and tall, gorgeous body—she wouldn't mind seeing him naked.

"Steve!" Her voice lifted and her excitement bubbled through. Thank God, talking to her foreman would take her mind off the man she should *not* be thinking about. "We've got a job and wait until you hear."

At home that afternoon, Bennett closeted himself in his office. The better to avoid his mother. She had a couple of her friends downstairs, looking through design books, God help him.

Desperate, he picked up the phone. When his sister answered, he said, "Damn it, Amanda, you have to help me!"

"Who is this?"

He glared at the phone. "Not funny."

"Sure it is," she said, laughing.

Bennett's grip tightened on his phone. "I don't see anything funny about this."

"That's because you have no sense of humor."

"Thanks. Thanks very much." Why had he considered for even a second that she would be on his side? Both she and Serena were enjoying his misery far too much to help him out of it.

"Mom and her pals are looking at paint samples and upholstery and… Damn it, stop laughing." Irritated beyond measure, Bennett walked to the wall of windows, then opened the French doors and stepped out onto the balcony to take in the ocean view. Here in Dana Point, the sea looked wild and seemed to stretch on forever. Ordinarily, that view calmed him down. Today it barely touched the tension coiled inside.

First a pixie with attitude giving him grief over rebuilding The Carey, and now his own mother making his home life a nightmare.

"Okay, now I'm feeling sorry for you," she admitted, "although your house could do with *something*."

"You haven't seen my house in five years."

"Yes, thanks so much for inviting me so often."

"Not what I'm talking about."

"Fine," she said, then asked, "Have you changed anything?"

"Of course not."

"And my point is made."

"*My* point is going unanswered. You and Henry have a giant house in Irvine. You could take Mom."

"I could, but I'm not going to," she said. "I love Mom, but she's obsessed with wedding plans. I don't need her on-site doing it."

"And you think I do?"

"You're not making wedding plans."

"That's not helpful."

"As helpful as you're going to get," she said.

"And *this* is why I will not be making wedding plans. Ever." Scowling out at the sea, he added, "Your species enjoy making mine miserable."

"Don't know what you're missing. You should talk to Henry," Amanda said, practically cooing. "He'll tell you how…happy he is."

Bennett closed his eyes, took a deep breath and said, "Please don't make me want to hurl. I don't need to know these things about my sisters."

"Your loss."

"Thank God."

"Bennett," she said on a sigh, "once she and Dad make up, your problems are over."

Sure, that was just right around the corner. His mother was settling in. Hell, she was *nesting*. In his house. "And have you seen signs of that happening?"

"Well, no…"

His father wouldn't give up the company and his mother was determined to make that happen, so there was no end in sight to the Retirement Wars. And apparently, Bennett was the one who would be paying.

"So I'm just supposed to give her free rein in my house?"

"She has excellent taste."

Yes, she did. Elegant. Understated. But hardly masculine. "It's not my style," he complained uselessly.

"Beige is no one's style, Bennett," his sister said.

"Fine. I'll try Serena."

She laughed again. "Good luck with that. There's not even room for Jack to move in there."

"Jack has that gigantic mansion in Laguna. Why aren't they living there?" Why was no one helping him?

"Because Serena wants to wait until they're married to live together. Trust me, Jack's not happy, either."

"Well, why would she do that?" It didn't make any sense. Now that she and Jack were back together and engaged, Serena was happier than she'd ever been,

"Because she wants Alli to get used to the idea first, and apparently Jack has to build a castle in the backyard."

"A *castle*?"

"Long story," Amanda said, then offered, "Why don't you try Justin?"

One hand clamped tight around the icy cold black iron railing surrounding his deck. Turning his face into the ocean wind, he felt irritation swell inside him. Their youngest brother had pretty much cut himself off from the family the last couple of years. And when he was being generous of mind, Bennett could admit, at least to himself, that he hadn't helped the situation any. But, damn it, Justin should be here. Involved.

At the very least, helping with the parental situation.

"Okay," Amanda allowed, "that was a cheap shot."

"Yeah. It was." He rubbed the spot between his eyebrows, and it did nothing for the ache settled there.

"Fine then, change of subject," Amanda said brightly. "Tell me more about the woman who's doing the job on The Carey."

"From one mess to another? That's a change of subject?" His mutter sounded pissy, even to himself.

"I looked her up," Amanda said, ignoring Bennett's bad mood. "She's got lots of great reviews."

And she looked far better in person than she did on her website. "I saw them."

"And the before and after pictures she's got on her website look fabulous."

"I saw them." He gritted his teeth and reached for patience that seemed, at the moment, elusive.

"What's she like?" Amanda asked. "You saw *her*, too."

"I did." And instantly, her image rose up in his mind. *Sexy pixie*, he thought, helplessly. Small, curvy, with bright green eyes and a wry twist to her mouth that intrigued him more than he'd like to admit. It was as if she was always laughing at some private joke. Or at him. When she looked up at him with that challenging stare, he'd felt something stir inside him. Lust, sure.

What man wouldn't have felt a tug, watching her move so efficiently around the room? He could see her making mental notes as she checked out the ravages of the fire. She was professional and sharp. But he couldn't seem to tear his gaze from the way those faded jeans of hers clung to her legs. From the small, firm breasts beneath her Yates Construction T-shirt. And when he caught a gleam in those emerald green eyes? Well, what she did to him was biology. And he was most definitely male.

But there was something more to her, too. Which he didn't want to think about. And that bothered him. No woman had caught his attention as quickly as she had. She was now officially an employee, and Bennett never mixed business with pleasure. But damned if he wasn't tempted anyway.

"So," Amanda said, "tell me about her."

What could he say that wouldn't set his sister off? "She's a smart-ass."

Amanda's whoop of laughter was so loud Bennett yanked his phone from his ear.

"I like her already," Amanda said finally.

"You would," he muttered, then said more loudly, "She seems competent."

"Wow, high praise."

Shaking his head, he gave a resigned chuckle. "Why did I call you again?"

"Because I'm your intelligent, insightful sister whose judgment you trust implicitly."

"Yeah, that's not it."

"A spark of humor from my brother, Mr. Stoic," she said with approval. "Hannah Yates is already a miracle worker."

"We'll see," he said, and watched the waves race toward the rocks beneath his house. Spray shot into the air over the roar of the water. He turned his back on the ocean, walked back into his office and took a seat behind his desk. And what was wrong with it, he wondered. Just like the one at Carey headquarters, it was steel and chrome and glass and did exactly what he needed it to do. But if it were up to his mother, God knew what his office would look like.

"She's only got four weeks to get the job done."

"She'll do it."

"You sound sure."

"Bennett," Amanda said, her tone serious now, "trust me on this. When a woman is in charge in what is essentially a man's territory, she does what she has to, to keep her word and get things done."

"The bonus I offered doesn't hurt, either," he said, though he had to admit, Amanda had a point.

"A hundred thousand?" She laughed again. "For that, I might have tried to pull it off!"

He smiled, in spite of himself. "I'll tell her if she needs help to call you."

"No thanks," she said. "My plate's already full. But Bennett…you're not going to do your hovering thing over the woman, are you?"

"What's that supposed to mean?"

"You know exactly what I mean. It's what you did to Serena when she first joined the company. What you try to do to Justin. What you do to me until I make you stop. You loom over people, making sure they're doing everything the way you want it done."

"How the hell else can I be sure they will?"

"Oh, I don't know, *trust*?"

The very idea of that was laughable. "This job is too important to take chances. I'll be checking in on her a lot."

"Checking *up*, you mean."

"Whatever."

"Good comeback."

"Amanda, if you're not going to help me get Mom off my back, just say so."

"Thought I already did," she quipped, then as if sensing he was going to hang up on her, she added, "Why don't you get her to show you the website she's got up for the Summer Stars program?"

"Why would I do that?" he muttered, raking one hand through his hair.

"Hovering," she said. "Or looming. Whichever. Anyway, the point being, while she's talking about what she's doing with the big contest, she's *not* redecorating your house."

She might be onto something, he told himself. And he should be keeping a closer eye on the Summer Stars program. The only reason he hadn't was that it had turned into his mother's baby, and he and Candace Carey had been spending entirely too much time together lately already.

The Summer Stars was a new and so far, *very* popular contest. Every year, the Carey Center held the Summer Sensation, a series of concerts spread out over three months. Everything from ballet to symphonies and plays was held in the palatial Center, but this year, Serena had come up with an idea to get the local community involved.

The Summer Stars program had been holding live auditions at the Center, recording them, then putting them on a website so people could vote for their favorite performers. Much like a reality TV show, the performer with the most votes would win and the grand prize was a summer performance night at the Carey Center.

Which was why he needed the restaurant up and running in four weeks. The grand prize winner would be there to be introduced to the public, the media and to be celebrated for their victory.

"Hellooo…"

"Yeah," he said, while Amanda's voice echoed in his ear. "I'm here. It's a good idea. I'll distract Mom tonight with talk of the contest."

"And make sure she's doing everything to your satisfaction?"

"Doesn't that go without saying?"

"You're hopeless," Amanda said, then hung up.

Bennett didn't think of himself as hopeless in any way. Instead, he was focused, determined, and right now that focus would be aimed directly at Hannah Yates. He tucked his phone into his pocket and stared out at the ocean again. But he wasn't seeing the blue of the sea or the windswept clouds scuttling across a diamond bright sky.

Instead, he saw the pixie as she laughed up at him. Hannah Yates.

He already felt in his bones that hiring her might have been a mistake.

Four

Hannah was at The Carey first thing in the morning. With the key in hand, she let herself in, hit the lights and paused just a moment to take in the wreckage. It wasn't the first place she'd seen, postfire. And still, she felt a tiny ping of regret that the beautiful old building had suffered such an indignity.

Picking her way through debris, she made her way to the kitchen and mentally made a list of what she wanted her guys working on when they arrived. Her dad was coming by, too, since, as he'd said, *For a hundred thousand dollars, the Careys get the whole Yates family.*

She'd be glad of his help. There was no better carpenter in California. What he couldn't fix or build from scratch hadn't been invented yet. If he had to, she had no doubt he could build a working car out of cedar.

"Hey, boss!" A shout from the front of the building. "You in here?"

"In the kitchen, Nick!" She turned and waited for her master plumber to walk through the door.

"What a mess," he muttered as soon as he did.

Short and barrel-chested, Nick boasted a full handlebar moustache that he swore his wife, Gina, loved more than him. He had a booming voice, a great laugh and magic hands.

"Damn shame," he went on. "I brought Gina here for dinner on her last birthday."

"Well," Hannah told him. "You can bring her back on her next birthday, too."

He nodded absently, then looked around again. "Want me to start the demo?"

"We'll wait for the others to get here." She opened a cabinet to show stacks of skillets and saucepots, and she had no doubt the others were just as full. "We could start emptying everything, though. Get a jump on it."

"Sure. Damn. I've never seen so many pans. Where do you want to stack it all?"

"For now, we'll use a couple of the tables in the main dining room," she said, and made another mental note to get some boxes in here. Or maybe just talk to King Carey. See if they were keeping all the cookware or getting new. A man who threw money around like he did, might not want dirty pans in his spanking new restaurant.

"Works for me. There's plenty of 'em out there." Nick bent down and grabbed a stack of skillets, bundling them up in his arms. He carried them into the other room and Hannah heard him call out a greeting.

"Hey, Mike, go on in there and start grabbing some of the pots and pans. And watch yourself. The damn things are heavier than they look."

Hannah was grabbing a handful of saucepans when Mike Holley strolled in. Young, seriously built and looked like a surfer. But he would be the first guy she'd call if she needed a roof repaired. Steve Scott, her foreman, came in right behind Mike, and the two of them entertained each other while they worked.

One by one, all of the guys arrived, with her father bringing up the rear, carrying a jug of coffee and a stack of paper cups.

"Found a way to keep me from bugging you about coffee, did you?" she asked.

Hank shrugged. "The boys'll appreciate it."

"Sure. The boys." To her father, even Carol and Tina were *the boys*. Shaking her head, because really, she never had been able to talk her father into anything he didn't want to do, she swept out one arm to encompass the restaurant and asked, "What do you think?"

"I think it's a damn mess," Hank said, turning in a slow circle to take it all in. "And I'm starting to think you're as crazy as the guy who hired you. What makes you think we can get this done in four weeks?"

Frowning, Hannah took another look around and had to admit, that it was going to be tight. Maybe too tight. But she would give it everything she—and her crew—had to make that deadline. "Dad, if you were still running the business, what would you have done with that offer Bennett Carey made?"

He took a deep breath, blew it out, winked and shrugged. "I'd have said yes just as fast as you did."

She grinned. "Thanks for admitting it."

"There's comfort in knowing we're both willing to take on a huge challenge?"

"Absolutely." Hannah leaned in, kissed his cheek and said, "The guys are in the kitchen, clearing everything out so we can start the demo."

"My favorite day on the job." Her father grinned. "As much as I love building things, there's nothing as much fun as demo day." He headed for the other room with a spring in his step.

Still smiling, Hannah turned toward the front door when it opened. All of the guys were here, so she couldn't imagine who—

Bennett Carey stepped into the room and looked

like the king she'd named him, standing in a barnyard. Completely out of place and yet, she thought… Somehow right at home, as well. But then, she told herself, men like Bennett Carey were always so confident, so sure of themselves that they seemed to fit in anywhere. Even if they looked—as he did at the moment—as if they'd rather be anywhere else.

Even knowing that, Hannah couldn't stop her heart from giving a hard jolt, or what felt like a buzz of sensation from dancing up and down her spine. Oh, she might be in some serious trouble here.

From the kitchen came the clashing symphony that symbolized a new job starting, and thankfully that was enough to shake her out of whatever state King Carey had put her in. Hammers, laughter, rock music pumping into the air and the shouts of men and women used to working together. Hannah had always loved the sound, but she watched Bennett wince at the noise.

"Sounds like you're wrecking the place not rebuilding," he said.

"You have to tear things down before you can rebuild," she pointed out.

"It wasn't down enough?" he muttered.

She smiled, then took a long moment to just look at him, and Hannah was forced to muffle a sigh of approval as nerves skittered through her. Backlit by a shaft of sunlight, he stood there motionless as if giving her the time to admire him.

So she did.

The dark blue suit, crisp white shirt and forest green tie he wore fit him as if made specifically for him. And it probably had been. His hair looked perfect, as well, and she took a mental pause, remembering what she looked like. She wore her faded blue jeans, a red Yates Construction T-shirt and her battered and much loved Doc Martens. Nothing she could do about her wardrobe even if she would, Hannah thought. She'd tried to change herself for a rich man once before, and she still regretted it. So Bennett Carey could take her as she was—or, she thought, even better, he could leave her alone to work.

Another crash from the kitchen and a burst of laughter splintered her thoughts. It was just as well. Sighing over a man she couldn't have was just pointless. "So what can I do for you, Mr. Carey?"

"I wanted to stop in and—"

"Check to make sure we were on the job?"

He scowled at her, and Hannah thought there must be something wrong with her because even that downward curl of his lips looked… Sexy.

"All right, yes. You don't have much time and—"

"And we know that," she finished for him. "We're on it. We're going to stay on it. I don't need a keeper."

"That's a shame because you have one," he said mildly, though the gleam in his eyes as he looked at her told her he wasn't *feeling* mild. "I'll be stopping in to check on your progress, so get used to it."

She shrugged and smiled. "You're not the first fluttery client I've had."

"*Fluttery*? Is that even a word?"

She nearly laughed at the insult stamped on his features, but somehow she managed to hold it back. She'd only said it to get a reaction from King Carey anyway.

"It's my word, so yes, it is. Besides, you know what I mean. The nervous types. Always worried, have to see for themselves."

He tucked the sides of his jacket back and slipped his hands into his slacks pockets.

"I'm not nervous." He looked around at the mess. "Although maybe I should be. What are all these pans and things here?"

"We emptied the kitchen cabinets. Put everything there until we know what you want to do with them."

"I don't want to do a thing with them." He blew out a breath. "I'll get John Henry to make that call."

"Great. That takes care of one problem."

"You're sure of yourself, aren't you?"

"Actually…" she said, glancing around the restaurant. She saw the debris, the destruction. And she knew that, like most of her clients, all Bennett Carey saw was the rubble. But she could see past all of that to what it was going to be. What she and her crew would do with it. They would bring it back from the darkness and let it live again—better than ever. When she looked back to him, she smiled and said, "Yes. I guess I am."

"I hope that confidence is well-placed," he told her. "I've got a lot on the line here."

"Yeah, me, too," she said, but he wasn't finished.

His gaze fixed on her, he said, "I'm taking a chance on you, Ms. Yates. You and your company."

Well, she felt the sting of that statement. Maybe it wasn't an actual insult, but it was damn close. "We do excellent work, and you know it or you wouldn't have hired us in the first place."

"As you pointed out yesterday, my options were limited."

"You arrogant—"

One eyebrow arched as if he were just waiting for her to give him a reason to fire her, and she wasn't going to give it to him. She didn't know what it was about this man, but apparently on very short acquaintance, he had discovered just how to push her buttons.

Holding up one hand, she said, "I'll apologize for that."

"Thank you."

"Even though you deserved it."

His mouth curved so slightly, it almost didn't qualify as movement. "Quite the apology."

"Look, if you're thinking you can insult me into quitting so you can hire someone else—"

"There is no one else, as you've already pointed out."

"There you go." She walked toward him and lifted

her gaze to his as she did. "So bottom line, we're all you've got. Luckily enough for you, we're worth every penny you're going to pay us. The Carey is going to be as beautiful as ever when we're finished with it. And just so you know, this job is important to me and my company."

"For the bonus."

A short, sharp laugh shot from her throat. "Damn straight for the bonus. Did you expect me to say the honor of working on The Carey would be enough?" It wasn't the "honor" of doing this job, it's what working for the Careys would do for her reputation. For her future. But she wasn't about to tell him that. "No. This job is important and it will be done to the high standards Yates Construction believes in."

"Good."

"It will be done quicker if you leave."

His lips twitched again, and she thought she even saw a flash of approval in his eyes before it was gone again.

"I'll go," he said, when another crash from the kitchen sounded out. He kept his gaze on hers as he added, "But I'll be back."

"Good movie."

"What?" He frowned, thought about what he'd just said and sighed. "Right. *Terminator.* Yes. Good movie. The statement stands. Get used to having me around, Ms. Yates—"

"Hannah."

He nodded. "Hannah. Get used to it because you'll be seeing a lot of me for the next few weeks."

She stared after him for a long moment after he left. Well, hell. Now she was looking forward to seeing him. And that was just dangerous. Gorgeous. Rich. Annoying.

What woman wouldn't be fascinated?

Damn it.

Bennett took two meetings after his run-in with Hannah Yates and for the first time in his life, had found it hard to concentrate. Which was completely unacceptable.

They had the Summer Sensation concert series nearly ready to begin and the voting on the Summer Stars was being tabulated. In two weeks, they'd announce the winner with a ton of media fanfare, and in four weeks, they'd have the reception and dinner at The Carey.

And there was Hannah Yates back in his mind again.

Absently, he looked around his office, taking in the huge space, with its chrome, steel, glass and black leather. The furnishings were sparse, but sleekly modern. There were abstract paintings on the walls and floor-to-ceiling tinted windows affording him a view of the world outside. His own desk was steel topped by glass with chrome accents. Even the desk phone looked futuristic in its slim silver casing.

As he looked around, he frowned as he suddenly realized that there wasn't a single soft space in the entire room. Why had he never noticed that before? Why was he noticing *now*?

Damn woman was splintering his thoughts about everything. Couldn't concentrate on meetings. Suddenly giving a damn what kind of furniture he had in his office. It had to be her. None of that had bothered him before Hannah Yates had entered his orbit.

He spun his desk chair around to stare out at the sunny skies beyond the glass and let his mind wander to that early morning visit to the restaurant.

She was so damn *tiny*. Yet every inch of her was packed with curves designed to drive a man crazy. Her jeans sculpted her legs and defined a butt that was world-class. Her T-shirt was tight enough to cling to her breasts and skim her narrow waist. That hair of hers. He'd always preferred long, blond hair on a woman, and yet, here he was, wondering how that short, inky black hair would feel in his hands.

Then there were her eyes. A pure, emerald green. Sharp. Cool. Dismissive and that really bugged him. Hell, women didn't dismiss Bennett Carey. But she did, with an amusement that was both irritating and intriguing.

He didn't hear his office door open, but closed his eyes on a heartfelt sigh when his father spoke up and ruined a perfectly good daydream.

"What's this about you canceling our cleaning contractor?"

Bennett had known this would be coming, and he'd braced for it, though now that the moment was here, irritation crawled through him. Turning around to face his father, Bennett said, "I found someone better."

"Better?" Martin bunched his fists at his sides. "We've had the Parris company for nearly twenty years."

"Yeah." Bennett stood up to face the man. "And they've been getting lazy, Dad. They're so sure of themselves and our contract with them, they've stopped giving us their best. It's been going on for the last two years."

"What has?"

"Slipshod work," Bennett told him. "They're not bothering to clean where they think it won't be noticed."

"You should have talked to them. Hell. To *me*," Martin argued. "We've got a longstanding relationship with those people."

"And they've been taking advantage of it. I've had complaints from some of the staff at the Center. I looked into it."

"Why didn't I hear about it?"

Boggy ground here, Bennett knew. "Because I'm the CEO, Dad."

Martin's features flushed with color, and Bennett knew the old man wasn't happy about being left out of the decision-making, but then he hadn't expected him to be.

"So it was time to shake things up," Bennett said flatly. "I've already got a top grade company contracted to take over as of this week."

"Who?"

Bennett looked down at his desk, checked the name to be sure, then lifted his gaze to his father. "Top of the Line. They come highly recommended, have a great reputation and they're 10 percent less expensive than Parris."

"So it's about money. You're saving some pennies—"

"Not pennies, Dad," Bennett interrupted. "And I wasn't the one who made the original suggestion to change companies."

"Who was? And why didn't I hear about any of this until the meeting?"

"Don Mackie, head of our in housecleaning staff, told me about the issues a month ago. I looked into it, talked to the head of Parris and, when that didn't change anything, I made the decision."

"Without me."

"Dad," Bennett said as calmly and quietly as he could manage, "I didn't ask for your opinion on this because it was straightforward and a good business decision."

"I don't like it," Martin muttered darkly.

"Change isn't always a bad thing, Dad." He had the distinct feeling his father was fighting retirement because Martin simply could not imagine not coming into the Carey offices every day. In a way, Bennett understood that. Martin didn't want to give up control, and Bennett was the same way. And that thought didn't bring him any comfort.

"Damn it, Bennett…" Martin pushed one hand through his gray-streaked hair and Bennett recognized the action as one he himself performed several times a day. Just how much like his father was he, anyway?

He loved his parents. But between his father refusing to let go of the reins of the company and his mother refusing to move out of Bennett's house… Well, even the tightest familial ties could get strained to the snapping point. And right now, he felt as taut as a rope strung across a chasm.

"Dad, I'm in charge of this company. From the big decisions to the smallest—like this one—it's up to me to make them."

"I'm not saying different," his father argued, though that's exactly what he'd been saying. "I simply think you should have told me yourself. Discussed it."

"Why?"

"Why?"

Bennett lifted one hand to shove at his hair, then let it drop to his side. "Because you put *me* in charge.

These decisions are mine to make now. Besides, it wasn't anything important, Dad. Not important enough to even warrant this conversation."

Martin's face flushed and his eyes snapped. "Is that right? You don't need the old man's opinion anymore, is that it?"

Sighing, Bennet said with a patience he hadn't thought he possessed, "Dad, you put me in charge for a reason. You knew I could do it and you knew it was time. What's changed?"

Scrubbing one hand across his face, Martin whirled around, took three or four steps away, then spun back. "I never considered what it would be like to be shut out. To *not* be in charge, and I damn well don't like it."

And that was the bottom line. Martin had spent his entire adult life building the Carey Corporation into the immense company it was today. Together with his wife, he'd raised four kids, trained them to take over and continue the Carey traditions. But now that it was time for that changing of the guard to happen, Martin couldn't bring himself to let go.

"Sorry to hear that Dad," Bennett said, and meant it. His father had built this company into a major player. He'd poured blood, sweat and tears into the making of it, and now that it was his turn to step back, he didn't know what to do with himself.

Bennett didn't even want to think about what it would be like when it was *his* turn. At least his father had a family. A wife who loved him enough to walk away from him in an attempt to wake him up.

What did Bennett have?

Instantly, the sexy pixie popped back into his mind and he ruthlessly pushed her aside.

"Your mother doesn't get it," Martin complained. "She thinks I should just walk away from everything I've spent my life building. Just turn my back and somehow magically not care what happens to it anymore."

"Dad, she knows you'll always care." Bennett shook his head. "What she wants to know is that you care just as much—or more—about *her*."

Martin's jaw dropped and his eyes bugged open. "That's ridiculous. Why the hell would she think I don't care about her? We're *married* for God's sake. We've got four grown kids, a granddaughter and nearly forty years together to show for it."

Wow. His father either really was clueless or he was deliberately not seeing the truth. Either way it had to stop. Soon.

"You know I'm not taking sides in this," Bennett said, feeling uncomfortable already. Hell, he'd spent the last several months avoiding getting dragged into the Retirement Wars. He could see his dad's point, but his mom had more on her side. Which was why he'd stayed out of it.

"Yeah, I know." He huffed out a breath. "What are you trying not to say?"

"Fine." Bennett came out from behind his desk, then leaned one hip against the heavy steel-and-glass slab. "I'm trying not to say that Mom's got a point. You promised her a lot when I took over, and you haven't delivered."

"What the hell kind of thing is that for my son to say?"

"You asked me to tell you."

"Well, I didn't want to hear *that*."

"This is why I stayed out of it."

"It was a good plan. Keep to it," Martin said.

"Wish I had," Bennett muttered.

"What was that?"

"Nothing." He took a breath, looked at his father and said, "Dad. Look. Mom's living with me because she's pissed at you."

"You could throw her out," Martin said slyly.

Bennett choked out a laugh. "Yeah, that's going to happen."

Scowling fiercely, the older man muttered, "Well, what should I do then if you won't help me?"

"Jeezz, Dad. You got her to marry you. Figure out what worked back then and do it again."

Martin gave him a long, thoughtful look.

Bennett walked back around his desk and dropped into the chair. "Just please do it somewhere else."

"That's a helluva thing to say to your father," Martin grumbled. "Fine. I'm going. And just so you know, I don't care about the cleaning company."

Bennett threw both hands up. "Then what was this all about?"

"To remind you that I'm not dead yet, Bennett. I'm still a part of this company." He stomped across the office and when he left, he slammed the door behind him hard enough to make one of the paintings on the wall tilt to the left.

Bennett sighed and let his head fall back against his chair. "Believe me, Dad. I know."

Five

By the third day on the job, they were hitting a rhythm.

Hannah was still worried, but feeling better about meeting the impossible deadline.

Tiny and Carol were working on replacing the beams in the attic while Mike was on the roof, pulling out the damaged shingles and roofing paper. Since he'd been able to find replacement shingles of the same style and color, they'd be able to patch the roof without having to replace the whole thing. Another time saver.

"Hannah! Can you come over here for a minute?"

Marco Benzi, late forties with brown eyes and a

perpetual three-day growth of beard on his cheeks, waved her over to where he stood beside an open fuse box.

"Is there a problem?"

"Not yet," he said, then tapped one of the old fuses. "This box is practically an antique."

She sighed. "Well, that's just perfect news."

"No, the good news is that the wiring in the building is safe."

"Um…the kitchen wasn't so safe."

"A short started that fire." He shook his head. "A spark was all it took. But the rest of the building checks out. Still. This thing's got to be replaced. It doesn't even have an RCD. That's asking for trouble."

Residual Current Devices were automatic protection devices in a fuse box. They contained switches that would trip a circuit under dangerous conditions and instantly disconnect the electricity. Preventing fires. Saving lives. If The Carey had had an updated fuse box before the fire, there might not have been one.

"Replace it all," she said. Hannah wasn't about to risk another fire in the building she was trying to save.

"On it, boss," Marco said, and went back to work, whistling under his breath.

One more thing, she thought, and had to admit that as a new problem, it was pretty small. Usually on a job, they found more complications than they'd been hired to fix. Rot under a floor. Water damage under a tub being replaced. All kinds of things could go wrong in a house or a business, and it was their job to fix it all. They were damn good at it.

"What's going on?"

Of course.

Hannah turned to look at King Carey, standing just inside the door. She should have been annoyed with his daily presence. Instead, she'd found herself watching for him. Waiting for him, a sense of expectancy coiled inside her.

This wasn't good, she told herself. Being attracted to the man was one thing, enjoying that attraction so much was something else. But then she'd been repeating that mantra since the moment she'd first met him. It didn't seem to help. All he had to do was walk into a room and she felt that now familiar buzz of a near electrical charge lighting up her body.

Hell. Maybe *she* needed an RCD.

"What's going on is work," she said. "Why aren't you off doing yours?"

"Because I had to stop in here first." He checked his watch, and she wondered absently just how many times a day he did that.

"Well, you're here now, so I'll show you around."

His eyebrows rose high on his forehead. "I wasn't expecting that."

"Well, good," she said. "I hate being predictable." She pointed to where Marco was working. "Starting there. Your fuse box is old and outdated. Not to mention dangerous. We're replacing it."

"Okay, good."

When she turned and waved at him to follow, he moved to do just that, stepping into the kitchen right behind her. In fact he was so close to her, Hannah could have sworn she felt the heat of his body pressing into her back. She closed her eyes briefly, took a breath meant to steady herself and, instead, all she managed was to inhale the scent of him. Sort of high-end woodsy. Like glamping, she thought with an inner smile.

"How do you know what you're doing in all of this?"

She looked around, trying to see it as he was. Cabinets torn out, counters ripped off and stacked neatly to one side. Appliances moved to what they were calling the storage area. Tarps on the old wood floors, gaping hole in the ceiling and smoke stains on drywall that had yet to be replaced.

"Actually, it looks good to me. We're making solid progress." She had to speak up over the clatter of noise the guys engendered. "Mike already checked the roof and the support beams. You're in good shape there. Whoever built this place so long ago was a craftsman."

"Good to know."

"Well, except for the wiring and that wasn't his fault. It was up to code sixty years ago." She shrugged. "Anyway, Mike's found replacement shingles, so we don't have to redo the whole roof."

"Also good news since we just did that two years ago," he told her.

She turned and looked up at him. "Tiny and Carol are working the attic, making sure there are no more scorched beams we haven't found yet."

He nodded and watched the hustle in the kitchen.

"Devin Colier is our flooring guy." Hannah used the toe of her boot to shove the tarp aside a bit. "You've got white oak here and it's solid. It's scraped and scarred from years of use and then the added excitement of the firemen and their tools and boots marking things up."

"They don't look good," he said as she dragged the protective tarp back into place.

"They will." She turned her face up to his and stared into his lake-blue eyes. How could a stern stare from him make her stomach spin and her breathing shallow and fast? Deliberately, she took a long, deep breath—taking the scent of him inside her again. He was really fogging up her mind. "Once the new cabinets are installed, Devin's going to come in and sand the floorboards, here and in the dining area."

"Shouldn't you be doing the floors before the cabinets?"

"Common misconception." Oooh. He didn't like the word *common*. "The subfloor is under the cabinets and that's already been replaced due to water damage from the firefighting. The finish flooring is what you'll see and walk on. And we want the kitchen and dining areas to match, so best we sand and stain all at once."

"Makes sense."

This was going way too smoothly, she thought. Where was the arguing? The demanding? Keeping a wary eye on him, she continued, "When that's done, he'll put a stain on." Tipping her head to one side, she asked, "Do you want a dark stain, like it was before? Or maybe a clear coat to let the grain of the wood shine through?"

One eyebrow lifted. "Judging by the way you said that, I know which choice you'd prefer. The clear coat. Is that your professional judgment?"

She shrugged. "A little, I guess. But more, it would look better, I think. Light floors, dark walls. Take some of the 'cave-like' feel of the restaurant away."

"Cave-like?"

He was insulted. She almost smiled because suddenly, they were back to normal.

Holding up both hands for peace, Hannah smiled. "Okay, I didn't mean to throw metaphorical darts at The Carey. But be honest. This place was built six decades ago, when dark cozy places reminded people of the Rat Pack or something. It probably felt… mysterious. Clandestine, even."

"Where do you get this stuff?" He honestly looked stunned.

Why did she so enjoy befuddling him? Probably because she had the feeling it didn't happen often. He was so in control. So studiously proper. "Doesn't matter. Just, trust me. It worked back then."

"It *still* works," he pointed out.

"Ah," she said, waving a finger at him. Again he looked at her as if he were trying to understand a foreign language. "But could it work even better? Times have changed. Moods have changed. Lightening up the restaurant, even this little bit? Gives it a whole new feel. Might bring in younger clientele, too."

Well, that put the scowl back on his face, and what did it say about her, that she preferred him that way? When he was being all calm and reasonable, she really didn't know what to make of him. Besides, that scowl of his was pretty damn sexy.

When he took the time to look around, both in the kitchen and the dining area, Hannah watched him. She could almost see him measuring, weighing his choices and even drawing what was probably a not very clear mental picture of what the finished restaurant would look like. Hannah could appreciate that. He wasn't only a sharp businessman, but he was open enough, willing enough, to consider something that hadn't been on his radar.

When he turned back to her, he nodded. "Go with

the clear coat. You might have a point about the place being too dark."

A slow satisfied smile curved her mouth. "Mr. Carey," she said. "There may be hope for you yet."

"That would depend," he said, "on what you're hoping for."

The flash of interest in his eyes kindled something inside her that she fought to ignore, because if she didn't, she might have to admit to what she was hoping for. And at the moment, that was to taste that scowling mouth of his.

So she laughed to cover what she was thinking, feeling, and said, "You never disappoint. And, I'd like to point out that we just had an actual conversation. No arguments. No sniping."

"The day is young," he retorted, then nodded, turned and walked out of the restaurant.

Hannah hated when he got the last word.

Bennett could not stop thinking about Hannah Yates, and that bothered him on several fronts. She wasn't the type of woman he was usually attracted to at all, yet, she was always at the edges of his mind.

"Bennett!"

He blinked like a man coming out of a dead sleep, and maybe he was. God knew, his mind kept drifting off to Hannah at the most inappropriate times. Like now, for instance. He stared at the man sitting across the desk from him.

Jack Colton, his sister Serena's fiancé and one of Bennett's oldest friends—also the head of the Colton Group, one of the largest hotel chains in the world. Jack's blue eyes were now watching him with amusement.

Well, that was annoying.

"What?"

"Good question," Jack said with a grin. "In the middle of talking about that castle I've got to get built in my backyard for Alli, you zone out. Where'd you go?"

"I'm right here," Bennett said, and sat forward, leaning both elbows on his desk.

"Sure, buddy." Jack leaned back in his chair and set his ankle on his knee. "So who is she?"

"I don't know what you're talking about."

"Right." He sat up straight, looked at the back of the steel and black leather chair. "These things are damned uncomfortable—did you know?"

"How would I know," Bennett said. "I don't sit in them."

"You should try them out," Jack told him as he stood up. "But not for long."

Frowning at the chairs, Bennett said, "They don't have to be comfortable. It's not like I want people to sit in here for hours."

"Then good job. Because I guarantee they won't."

Jack was the first person—beyond his sisters—to complain about his office furniture. And maybe, he admitted silently, Jack had a point. Sighing, Bennett asked, "Was there a reason for your visit today?"

His friend laughed shortly. "Good to see you, too."

Pushing one hand through his hair, Bennett swung his chair to one side and tapped his fingers on his desk. "Fine. You want to talk, we'll talk. What's going on? Serena driving you crazy with wedding plans? Because she and Amanda both are doing that to the rest of us. Seems only fair that you have to pay since you're the one who asked her."

Jack slapped one hand to his chest and grinned. "Damn, Bennett, that was so touching."

"What do you want, Jack?"

"I want names." Jack started walking, doing a circuit of the office, turning his head to look back at Bennett.

"Names?" Bennett repeated. "Why? Is Serena pregnant?"

Jack shook his head. "Not yet, and that's not what I meant. You know I promised Alli a castle in the backyard at my house."

"Yeah…and a puppy, Serena says."

"True. But castle first, puppy after," Jack said, and stopped at the windows to take a long look out at the sun-splashed business park. When he turned to Bennett again, he said, "I've been living in Europe for seven years. I have no idea who to call for this. I thought you might have a couple of names of contractors."

Bennett went very still, then narrowed his gaze on the other man. "This is a setup, right? Serena told you about Hannah Yates."

"Of course she did," Jack said with a laugh. "Doesn't mean my question's not valid. I need a contractor. So, is she any good? Could she do it?"

"Probably. But she's not doing anything but the restaurant for the next three and a half weeks."

"Understood," Jack said. "But she could take a look at the yard, give me some ideas."

"I suppose that'd be all right."

"Damn, Bennett, do you have every minute of her day accounted for?"

"Just for the next three and a half weeks. And I don't want her distracted from the job."

"Don't want her distracted," Jack repeated. "Is work all you think about Bennett?"

"What's that supposed to mean?"

"I think it's pretty clear," Jack said with a shake of his head. "When I look at you, I see me not too long ago and it's not good."

"I don't have time to be analyzed, Jack."

Jack pushed the edges of his jacket back and shoved his hands into his pockets. Shaking his head, he said, "Bennett, we've been friends for a long time."

"Yeah, so?"

"So, I'm wondering when you're finally going to loosen up."

"Loosen up?"

"Yeah." Jack looked at him. "You're so tied up in the company, you don't have a life any more than I did until I found Serena again."

Insulted, Bennett said, "Says the man who just spent the last seven years rebuilding his family's company. You call that 'loose'?"

"No." Pulling his hands free, Jack walked closer. "You're right. I did spend almost every waking hour working or thinking about the company. Then I noticed work was all I had. And maybe you've noticed that I've done some substantial loosening since I moved back to California."

"I noticed you have the time to stop by my office to insult me."

"See? Exactly. You have to make time for the important stuff."

A short bark of laughter shot unexpectedly from Bennett's throat. "So it's important to insult me. Great. Thanks for that."

"No problem." Jack smiled to soften the words, but still, he said, "Bennett, you spend too much time here. Hell, you're trying to get your dad to walk away, but you're here more than he is."

"This is my job."

"This is your *life*," Jack countered. "And if you're not careful, it's going to be all you've got."

"And suddenly you have the answer to life?" Bennett snorted. "You're wasting your time in the hotel industry. You should be a therapist."

"Don't have the patience for it," Jack admitted. "Just standing here trying to pound sense into your hard head has pushed me to my edge."

"Then step back," Bennett told him. "I don't have a problem. I have a company that needs me. And I'm trying to get my father out because he retired!"

"And is that how long it's going to take to get you to leave?"

Why was everyone so worried all of a sudden about how tightly wound he was or wasn't? His sisters were on him. His mother. Hell, even Hannah Yates had voiced her opinion. And now his friends were jumping on the bandwagon?

Bennett didn't overwork. He worked just enough. He kept tabs on his employees, on his company, on his family members. He had a home. He didn't sleep in his office, for God's sake. Of course, he was forced to admit, he wasn't home much. Less, now that his mother had set up camp there. But that didn't mean he didn't have a life.

"I *like* my life," he muttered darkly.

"Yeah? Why?"

"Why should I have to define that for you?"

"The question is *can* you define why?"

He shot Jack a hard glare. "Because it's the life I built. The one I want. You don't have to live it so what do you care?"

"You're my friend. Soon to be my brother-in-law."

"And?"

"And, I'd like to see you sometimes without having to come to the office to do it." Jack scrubbed one hand across the back of his neck. "Hell, Serena and I invited you to dinner a few nights ago, and you were *here.* Going over some problem with marketing."

All right, yes, he might spend too much time at the company, but in his defense, "Serena can't cook."

Jack laughed as he was meant to. "I was grilling and you missed a good meal with us and with Alli."

Bennett hated it when he was wrong. Thankfully, he told himself, it didn't happen often. But this time, was one of the rare occasions. He should have gone to dinner at Jack's place in Laguna. Bennett hadn't seen much of his niece, Alli, lately, and he missed her.

"I was like you," Jack said. "Until I came back. Until Serena and I reconnected. Now I can see how little my life mattered before."

Bennett buried his impatience and the small bubble of anger that had begun to form. Jack was his friend, and even if Bennett didn't like what the man was saying, he understood where it was coming from. "I get what you're trying to do, Jack. And I should appreciate the thought anyway. But I'm not interested in getting married. I don't—"

"Have the time?" Jack finished for him.

"Funny." He checked his watch. There were still two hours until his next appointment. Standing up, he buttoned his suit jacket. "I'll tell you what. I'm willing to leave the office right now. I'll take you by The Carey. You can meet Hannah Yates and see if she's the contractor for you."

Jack smiled. "You're willing to take off work in the middle of the day to go by the restaurant, *just* to introduce me to your contractor."

Bennett stared at him. "You have a problem with that?"

"Nope I just find it…interesting."

Interesting. Bennett could live with that; he just hoped that his old friend couldn't see that he was really looking forward to seeing Hannah Yates again. Which he didn't want to think about, either.

Hannah felt a disturbance in the force the instant that Bennett Carey entered the restaurant.

She should have been used to it by then, but she wasn't. His spontaneous visits had caused her to be constantly on edge. Waiting for him to walk through the door. And the minute he did, every nerve in her body went on high alert.

Tossing a glance over her shoulder at the crew behind her, she walked into the main dining room to see Bennett and another man with him. She hardly spared the stranger a quick look before focusing on the man she couldn't stop thinking about.

"You're late," she said when her heart dropped out of her throat.

"What?"

"Well, check that famous watch of yours," Hannah teased. "It will show you that you're at least an hour behind when you usually stop by to check on me."

He frowned and Hannah grinned. Walking up to the other man, she held out one hand. "Hannah Yates."

"Jack Colton," he said, and when he released her hand, he looked around the scene. "I know you're working on it, but right now it's…"

"A mess," she said. "But it won't be for long." Turning to Bennett, she added, "John Henry phoned and told me to donate the kitchen counters and the old skillets and pans. He said he'll be expecting a new supply to go with his new kitchen."

"Of course he did," Bennett mused.

"Well, we donated the counters to Habitat for Humanity and the pans to the Goodwill, then broke down the damaged tables. We're building new ones and I thought you might want to consider a couple of longer tables surrounded by banquettes in the back there." She pointed, and the two men turned to look. "Most of the tables are, as you know, round and sufficient for four to six people. But if The Carey's being remade, I thought you might want to allocate some space here for larger gatherings.

"You know, family celebrations, business meetings…" She smiled when he flicked a look in her direction. "If you okay the idea, my dad and another of our crew will build the tables and then construct the banquettes around them. I'm thinking, cream-colored leather for the booths and chairs. What do you think?"

"Wow." Jack grinned and nodded. "I think you might even beat out Bennett's sister Amanda at how many words you can get out in one long breath."

She smiled at him, then shifted her focus to where it wanted to be. Bennett. The fact that he was watching her made her feel warm from head to toe. She steadied herself and said, "I've learned that if I want something, it's easier if I just lay it all out at once."

"Easier on me?" Bennett asked.

She nodded. "That way you only have to get mad once and we're finished."

Jack laughed again, but she hardly heard him. All she could see was Bennett. His gaze locked with hers, and she swore she could see actual flames in those bright blue eyes. Or maybe, she considered, it was the fire inside her being reflected in his eyes.

"Yeah." Jack looked from one to the other of them, then said, "If you don't mind, I'm just going to walk into the kitchen, see what they're doing…"

She hardly noted when he left. Instead, she kept her gaze on Bennett. "Brought a friend with you to help you keep tabs?"

His mouth curved slightly. "Oh, I don't need help."

"Agreed. You seem pretty good at it."

"Well, I've had a lot of practice."

Now her mouth curved. What was it about him? He hovered. He gave unwanted advice. Pronounced orders with that kingly attitude. And yet… Here she was, wondering what that mouth tasted like. Wondering how his hands would feel on her skin. Wondering—

"It's a mess in there, too," Jack announced as he came back into the room. "But it looks like they all know what they're doing."

"That's what I've been trying to tell Mr. Carey."

"I'll tell him for you."

She threw him a quick smile. "It's appreciated."

"He knows as much about construction as I do," Bennett said. "Which is nothing."

"It hasn't stopped you from telling us what to do and how to do it," she reminded him.

"I know how to motivate people."

"By browbeating them?"

"I haven't touched your brow."

"Metaphorical brows."

"As fascinating as this is," Jack interrupted, "I came here to meet you and to ask if you could build a castle."

Well, that got her attention. "A castle? I suppose we could. If we have about ten years and a lot of stone."

He grinned, glanced at Bennett and said, "I like her." Then to Hannah, he added, "A child-sized castle. In my backyard. For my soon-to-be stepdaughter."

"Oh." Her smile was wide and open. "I love that. What a fun idea. I'd love to talk to you about it—"

"In three and a half weeks," Bennett ground out.

She slid her gaze back to him. "I can talk about other jobs while doing one job."

"Multitasking." Jack nodded. "Serena's always telling me that women are stars at multitasking."

"I'm not paying you to multitask," Bennett reminded her, ignoring Jack.

"You'll get what you paid for, Mr. Carey," she said, then looked at Jack. "And when it's finished, we would love to build a castle for you, Mr. Colton."

"Jack, please."

She smiled and nodded. Then when she looked to Bennett again, she felt the smile slowly slide away. "Now, if you'll excuse me, I'll get back to work before you have to check your gold watch and decide if I'm wasting time or not."

Hannah heard Jack laugh as she left the room, but she *felt* Bennett Carey simmering.

Good. So was she.

Six

Hannah hadn't seen Bennett Carey in three days. Not since he'd stopped by the restaurant with his friend Jack Colton.

And she'd Googled Colton. Head of the Colton Group of hotels. Just as she had hoped, doing this job for the Careys was going to lead Yates Construction into other jobs. Sure, building a backyard castle wasn't exactly a huge assignment, but if Jack Colton liked it, he might use her company on jobs for his hotels. Or his house. Or maybe it would be an introduction to someone else. This was just the first of what she knew would be many jobs to come their way.

The first week working on The Carey had gone

fast. So fast that Hannah had stayed up nights making notes, juggling their other jobs and worrying about that four-week deadline. Last night, she'd added in researching castles to get an idea of what Jack Colton might eventually want.

Having Bennett Carey continually "dropping by" the restaurant to check on their progress wasn't helping anything, either. This was the most important job they'd ever had, but it was hard to concentrate on construction when King Carey was constantly popping up and shattering her focus.

How could she consider floor joists or drywall, when her brain kept drifting to Bennett Carey's eyes. Or his big hands. Or how she wanted to nibble on his bottom lip for an hour or two?

She carried her first cup of coffee out of the kitchen to the front porch, where she sat on the cedar glider her father built for her when she bought the tiny house in Long Beach. Two years she'd lived there, and it still wasn't what she wanted it to be. What she knew it could be. She'd done the basic remodel, first on the bathroom that had held the smallest tub she'd ever seen. She'd expanded the room, installed a glorious soaker tub that she enjoyed every night, new lighting, new vanity and an oil-rubbed, bronze vessel sink. Along with the walk-in, hand tiled shower, her bathroom now was like taking a vacation in a five-star spa.

The kitchen, however, still looked as it had in the fifties.

"I'll get around to it," she assured herself, settling against the plump pillows stacked on the glider. There would be time for all of it, and extra money once she'd finished the restaurant job.

Six in the morning, the narrow street was quiet but for a few neighbors firing up their cars for the drive to work. The sun was rising and spreading a soft pink across the sky, and Hannah took a moment to simply *enjoy* this time. Every morning, she sat on this glider and thought about the day ahead, making mental notes for the hours to come.

Since she spent her days with the sounds of power tools and loud men shouting and laughing, she relished this slice of silence that started her mornings. She curled her legs up under her, cradled the mug between her palms and sighed a little.

This house, with its wide front porch had called to her the moment she'd seen it. Small, forgotten, allowed to fall—not apart, but asleep. Hannah was slowly waking it up, making it what it had been when it was first built in the fifties. Actually, making it more. She loved it.

But at the moment, she only wanted to enjoy this time alone. These few minutes every morning gave Hannah the center she needed to handle the job, the crew and any problem that popped up.

"Like for example," she muttered, "*this* one."

A gleaming black BMW parked in front of her house, and even before the driver stepped out, she knew who it was. Who else did she know who could afford a car like that?

"Why is King Carey here to ruin my morning?"

He shut the car door and took a long moment to study her house as he would some ancient archeological dig. As if trying to figure out why anyone would want to live there.

"Perfect." She refused to give up her seat on the glider, so she called out, "Isn't this a little early for you?"

His gaze snapped to her, and Hannah could have sworn she felt a jolt of heat shoot right through her. She swallowed hard, then took another sip of coffee, more to keep busy as he stalked up the stone walkway than because she wanted it.

He wore a black suit, black shirt and a tie the color of blood. If he was headed to a meeting, he was going to scare the crap out of his adversary. He didn't scare her, though. What he did to her was better left undefined.

"What're you doing here?" she asked, then held up a hand before he could answer. "No, how did you find out where I live?"

He leaned one shoulder against the porch post, then thought better of it and pushed away. Brushing one hand over his suit jacket to rid himself of dust—or, Hannah thought, *cooties*—he looked at her.

What was it about him that drew her in, she wondered. All week at the job, whenever he stopped by, she had felt his presence before she actually saw him. It was as if the air charged around him and sent her signals by the zip in her blood and the tingling in every one of her nerve endings. Yes, he was gorgeous. But it wasn't just his looks that pulled at her.

It was that constant scowl, the impatient gleam in his eyes and the oh-so-rare half smile that surprised her every now and then. All she knew was that she thought about him when he wasn't there, dreamed about him at night and really resented the hell out of the fact that another rich man was making her think things she shouldn't.

She'd been down this road before, and she knew it ended badly. So why was she allowing herself to repeat her own history? Internally warning herself to get a grip, she paid attention when he started speaking.

"Finding where you lived was difficult. I employed a private detective named Google."

She grinned. There it was again, that unexpected humor that threw her just a little off-balance. "Wow. Was that a joke?"

"Is it so surprising?"

"Actually, yes." She grinned up at him and wasn't surprised when he shifted his gaze away to look around the porch.

She knew what he was seeing. A long, concrete

porch, painted a bright yellow with white trim. She had to guess that it was little to nothing like the palace he no doubt lived in.

"Looking for something?".

"What?" His gaze snapped to her. "No."

Sighing, Hannah scooted back on the glider and patted the sky blue-and-yellow-flowered cushion beside her. "Have a seat."

He glanced at the glider, and she could almost *see* the distaste on his face. Her first instinct was to be offended, but she let that go quickly. She couldn't really blame him. He looked as out of place here as she would in one of his board meetings. Hannah had the feeling he didn't do a lot of front porch sitting. And maybe he needed to.

"It doesn't bite," she offered.

"Can you be sure?"

"More humor. A red-letter day." Why did she find that so enticing? Maybe because she knew it was very nearly a gift, these rare peeks at a man who was ordinarily so stiff and stern and all business? Did he ever unwind? Did he sleep in a suit? Was it his birthday suit? Oh, the images that raced through her mind.

He gingerly sat down beside her and frowned at the glider's movement. "Never saw the appeal in rocking chairs."

"It's a glider," she corrected.

"What's the difference?"

"This glides," she pointed out, giving him a half smile. "Rockers rock."

"Whichever." He looked at her. "Why would you want your chair to move?"

"A question for the ages," she muttered. He looked so stiff. So uncomfortable, she nearly laughed. Then she remembered that he had shattered her morning routine and was now, instead of just showing up at the job site, appearing at her house. At the crack of dawn. Across the street, the Morrison family was up and moving. She could tell because in a blink, nearly every light in the house snapped on. Three houses down from them, the light on Doc Burns's front porch clicked off as the older man carried his golf clubs out to his car.

Morning was creeping in, and families up and down the street were beginning to stir.

And it occurred to her that Bennett Carey really didn't belong in her everyday world. A damn shame because she *really* liked looking at him.

"Back to my original question," she said finally, when she turned to look at the tall gorgeous statue sitting beside her. She took a sip of coffee as he stared at her. "What are you doing here?"

He pushed the sleeve of his jacket back and checked that gold watch of his. Wound seriously too tight. His schedule seemed to rule him rather than the other way around, and Hannah had the urge to snap him out of his well-trod rut. At the moment though, she was trying to ignore the flutter of something fabulous happening inside her. He was so close, she could smell his aftershave and feel the heat lifting off his body.

So close, she could reach out and run her hand through his hair. She cupped her fingers more tightly around her coffee cup.

"I've got an early meeting in Los Angeles," he said, "so I won't be able to stop by the restaurant today."

She clucked her tongue. "How will we get by without you?"

His lips twitched. Another sign of humor, and she had to wonder if he knew just what that slight smile did to her. Probably not. If he did, he wouldn't do it.

"Entertaining," he said, then added, "I figured you would be up this early since you're usually at the restaurant by eight."

Wow. Not only did he have his schedule memorized, but hers, too. "Your stalking is very efficient."

"I'm not stalking you, I'm…keeping tabs on you."

She lifted her coffee cup in a toast. "Interesting definition of hovering."

"Stalking. Now hovering?" He shook his head. "I'm the one paying for this job. I'm the one who needs it done."

"Then maybe you're the one who should give us the space to do it."

He pushed off the glider, sending her into a hard

back and forth. She didn't move to stop it, only stared at him over the lip of her mug.

He pushed his jacket aside and shoved his hands into his pockets. How could he look so irritated and so…tempting all at the same time? She knew it was a mistake to indulge herself with private fantasies of what could happen between the two of them. It splintered her focus and at the same time, set her up for disaster if she ever allowed herself to *actually* indulge.

"I took a chance on you and your company."

Okay, that got Hannah to her feet. Setting the coffee cup down on the porch railing, she tipped her head back to glare at him and, not for the first time in her life, wished she were five or six inches taller.

"I run a damn good company and you know it," she said, stabbing her index finger at him for emphasis. "And you didn't give us this job out of some generosity of spirit. You had no choice but to 'take a chance' just like I'm taking a chance on you."

A short bark of laughter shot from his throat. "Some chance. You're being paid very well."

"And you're getting your restaurant back in better shape than it was before the fire and in record time. So I guess we're both happy."

He shook his head, whether in admiration or exasperation, she couldn't be sure. Then he spoke and all questions ended.

"You are the most infuriating woman I've ever known."

"I'm both flattered and annoyed," she said. "And right back at you."

"Me?" He was clearly shocked. "How am I infuriating?"

"Oh, I don't know." She tossed both hands high. "The constant checking up on me for instance? Constantly questioning my competence. Checking your watch every other second? Dropping by the job site at all times of the day."

"My restaurant."

"My job site."

Something simmered in the air between them as it had been for the last week. She was almost getting accustomed to the sizzle and burn inside her. God knew, she actually looked forward to it now. For several long seconds the air felt electrified as they stared at each other.

Then he checked his watch again.

"Oh for heaven's sake. You should get rid of that watch."

He snorted. "Not likely. I've got appointments to keep and I'm never late."

"Never?"

"Never." He threw that last word down like it was a trophy he'd earned for being OCD.

"And do you still have time to make your meeting this morning?"

"Not if I don't get on the damn freeway soon."

She grabbed her coffee and sat down on the glider again, even though she knew that recapturing the peace of her private sunrise was futile. Even after he left, his presence would haunt her. Make her remember the sweep of nerves jangling through her whenever he was close. Didn't seem to matter that he could make her so angry.

Right from the beginning, she'd enjoyed his irritability. More than enjoyed—it almost fed the attraction for Hannah. What fun was any kind of relationship if it was always… Nice?

But all she said was, "Well, fly free. Don't let me keep you."

"Like I said," he muttered. "Infuriating."

She toasted him with her coffee again and thought about how she was glad to sit down, since being that close to King Carey always made her knees weak.

"Look," he said after a long, deep breath, "the main reason I stopped by was to tell you that John Henry is going to stop in to see you today. He has a list of changes he wants made in the kitchen and I wanted you to know that whatever he wants, he gets."

Her eyebrows rose. "He must be important to you."

"One of my best friends. But more than that, he's the best chef in California and I plan on keeping him."

"Well, free rein in a kitchen design should do it for you." She took a sip of her now cold coffee. "But you could have called me with that command."

"Yeah," he admitted, staring across the street when one of the Morrison boys raced out to a van and started an engine that desperately needed a muffler. Looking back at her, he said, "I could have. Should have."

Intrigued, she asked, "Why didn't you?"

It took him a second or two of thoughtful silence before he blurted out, "I decided I wanted to see you. Away from the job site." He didn't look happy about that. "Obviously I'm a secret masochist."

She laughed and felt something stir inside her. Yes, she was definitely intrigued by tall, dark and grumpy. "Obviously. Okay another question."

"Sure, why not?"

"How many suits do you own?"

"What?" He scowled at her. "What does that have to do with anything?"

"It's just a question, Mr. Carey."

"Bennett."

She nodded and swallowed hard against another rising swirl of nerves. "Bennett." Pausing, Hannah studied him and thought about it for a second. "You know, I think that's too stuffy. I'll call you Ben."

He frowned. "No one calls me Ben."

"No one? Not even your family?"

"No one," he repeated.

"Well, that's even better," she said lightly, beginning to enjoy herself immensely. "So how many, Ben? Suits."

Still scowling, he admitted, "I have no idea."

"Uh-huh." She stood up, set her mug down on the railing again and asked, "How many pairs of jeans?"

"Two."

She grinned at his quick response. "This is why you need me to call you Ben. Seriously wound too tight."

"I'm getting very tired of hearing that." His lips thinned and a muscle in his jaw twitched as if he were grinding his teeth to keep whatever else it was he wanted to say from spilling out. Then he blurted out, "Does that engine sound off like that every morning?"

Funny, Hannah thought. She'd stopped hearing the loud roar from the car. As she thought it, the boy drove off in a symphony of thunderous noises, and when it was quiet again, she looked up at him and said, "Yes."

"My God. Why hasn't the neighborhood taken up a collection to buy him something different?"

"Because he's a kid and he loves that van."

"No accounting for taste," he mumbled.

"No," she agreed, "there really isn't. Which leads me to this." It was spur-of-the-moment, completely. Maybe it was thinking of him as Ben rather than Bennett. Made him more… Approachable, though no less dangerous. And still, she couldn't resist one little taste.

She went up on her toes, grabbed his suitcoat lapels and pulled him down to her, then laid her mouth on his for three or four long, lingering seconds. One taste, she reminded herself, though oh, how she wanted more. Heat roared through her. Every nerve ending stood up and applauded. Her stomach did a wild roll and spin, and when she let him go, she grabbed the porch railing just to stay steady.

Then she looked up into his eyes and saw heat flashing in the dark blue. "What was that?" he asked.

"That was a kiss."

"Why?"

"I'm not sure," she admitted, cocking her head to study his features as if she'd never seen him before. "I guess, you looked like you needed to be kissed."

"Is that right?" He moved in closer. "And did you need to be kissed, as well?"

"*Need* is a strong word…" God, what had she been thinking? She'd been down this road before. With an über-rich, handsome man who had so little in common with her it was laughable until it all went to hell. And this time, the very rich man could make or break her company.

"*Need*," he said, "is a very strong word, and it almost captures what's happening right now."

"Yeah," she said, and took a step back. It seemed cowardly, even to her, but somehow she couldn't quite stop herself.

Meanwhile, the sky brightened and birds started singing in the trees. Down the street, another car started its engine and the throaty purr sounded like a heartbeat racing as fast as her own.

"I think you might be onto something," he murmured.

"What are you talking about?"

"It's what *you* were talking about. *Need*," he repeated, and that single word seemed to reverberate throughout her body, like a plucked harp string, vibrating on and on.

"Uh-huh." Hannah took a deep breath, hoping to steady herself, and though it didn't work, she pretended it had. "Well, you should probably get on the freeway or you'll be late."

"Probably, and as I said, I'm never late," he said. "And yet, I'm not ready to leave."

"Why not?"

"Because now it's you who looks as if she needs something."

Oh God. She knew exactly what she needed. Wanted. Was it so easy to read on her face? If it was, she wouldn't address it. Instead, she went for a lighthearted response. "Coffee? A little peace and quiet? Solitude?"

"None of the above."

"Really?"

"Really." He set his hands at her waist and lifted her off her feet to plant a kiss on her that Hannah swore set her hair on fire.

Her brain simply scrambled. Her blood burned and her heartbeat raced so loudly, it sounded like a drumbeat in her own ears. For what felt like forever,

Get up to 4 FREE FABULOUS BOOKS You Love!

To thank you for being a loyal reader we'd like to send you up to 4 FREE BOOKS, absolutely free.

Just write "YES" on the Loyal Reader Voucher and we'll send you up to 4 Free Books and Free Mystery Gifts, altogether worth over $20, as a way of saying thank you for being a loyal reader.

Try **Harlequin® Desire** books featuring the worlds of the American elite with juicy plot twists, delicious sensuality and intriguing scandal.

Try **Harlequin Presents®** Larger-print books featuring the glamourous lives of royals and billionaires in a world of exotic locations, where passion knows no bounds.

Or **TRY BOTH!**

We are so glad you love the books as much as we do and can't wait to send you great new books.

So don't miss out, return your Loyal Reader Voucher Today!

Pam Powers

LOYAL READER
FREE BOOKS VOUCHER

YES! I Love Reading, please send me up to 4 FREE BOOKS and Free Mystery Gifts from the series I select.

Just write in "YES" on the dotted line below then return this card today and we'll send your free books & gifts asap!

➡ YES ⬅
– – – –

Which do you prefer?

☐ **Harlequin Desire®**
225/326 HDL GRGA

☐ **Harlequin Presents® Larger Print**
176/376 HDL GRGA

☐ **BOTH**
225/326 & 176/376
HDL GRGM

FIRST NAME

LAST NAME

ADDRESS

APT.#

CITY

STATE/PROV.

ZIP/POSTAL CODE

EMAIL ☐ Please check this box if you would like to receive newsletters and promotional emails from Harlequin Enterprises ULC and its affiliates. You can unsubscribe anytime.

HD/HP-520-LR21

his mouth took hers. His lips, tongue, teeth, played and demanded and gave all at once.

Hannah sank into what he was doing to her. So many sensations rushed through her at once Hannah felt as if her head was about to fly off her shoulders and she wouldn't have cared. She'd never experienced anything like this, and that one small kiss she'd given him was like a sparkler next to this wild explosion of taste, scent, touch. Every inch of her body lit up like a Christmas tree, and she dug her hands into his shoulders to hold on and savor every second.

And just when she was considering crawling up his body like scaling a mountain, he let her go and took a step back.

A little dizzy, a lot horny, she could only blink and stare up at the man who had worked her up just to let her go.

"What?"

He shook his head, scrubbed one hand across his jaw. Then he fired a hard glare at her, as if leaving her achy and wanting was *her* fault.

"I have to go."

"Of course you do." Hannah's breath charged in and out of her lungs, but she felt a bit better when she noticed that he wasn't in much better shape than she was. Her knees were wobbly and the fog over her brain had barely lifted. She still felt… *Otherwhere*. And yeah, she knew that wasn't a real word, but it was the only thing she could think of to describe the feelings racing through her.

He checked his watch.

Hannah wanted to rip that gold watch off his wrist and throw it as far as she could. It would be good for him. And great for her.

"I have a meeting," he repeated.

"So you said. Well. Can't be late."

"No."

"Great. Go. Happy trails." Damned if she'd let him see what he'd done to her.

"Fine. We both have jobs to do."

Wow. He looked as if he wasn't sure what to say, so he fell back on his standard grim expression and crabby, kingly manner. How did a man go from insanely hot to cool and calm in seconds? Did he have some internal switch he could flip when he strayed too far off his normal routine?

Hannah grabbed her coffee cup off the porch rail, walked past him and opened the front door. She gave him a quick look over her shoulder. "Have fun on the freeway. I hope there's traffic."

She shut the door while he was still looking at her and when she was safely inside, felt one small swell of satisfaction. Hannah Yates had nearly crushed King Carey's blasted schedule. And she knew that while he raced to the freeway to make his meeting, his mind would be filled with thoughts of her.

Seven

As promised, John Henry Mitchell showed up on-site about noon, and Hannah liked him right away. He was so tall he made her feel even shorter than usual. But he had a wide smile and an easy manner that was refreshing after dealing with Bennett Carey.

"It's coming along," the man said as she showed him around the kitchen.

She looked up at him and grinned. "I know it doesn't look like much, but we've got most of the stuff you'll never see finished already." She waved one hand at the wall where the fire had started. The drywall had been pulled off to display the two-by-fours that made up the framing and the new wiring. "Our electrician has completely changed out the old wiring so you'll never have to worry about that again."

"Good to hear," John Henry said, stuffing his hands into the pockets of his black jeans. "That's not something I want to see again in my lifetime."

"Don't blame you." Hannah steered him to one side of the kitchen to the walk-in pantry. "We've added shelves in here, expanding your storage capabilities," she said, waving one hand to encompass the walls inside.

"That's great," he said, smiling down at her. "It was one of the things I wanted to ask for."

Hannah grinned. "Happy to help. I was thinking you might want a few big bins at the back of the pantry. For storage."

"Good idea." He stepped out and looked at the old freezer. "What about the freezer? Anything you can do with that?"

"We're going to add more shelving and lights. It seems a little dark in there."

"Dark enough that I use a flashlight most days."

She laughed. "I could tear it out and install a new one, but if you want my opinion…"

"I do."

Nodding, she continued. "That's a top-of-the-line freezer. Granted it's twenty years old, but it's still in great shape. I could have our plumber come in and check it out, maybe give the motor a tune-up and make sure the flooring is as good as I think it is. Then we'll add more storage, the new lights and leave the rest of it alone."

"Sounds good." He turned to face the main room and ignored the crew hard at work and the sounds of hammers, saws and a radio currently tuned to a country station. "My real concern," he said, "is with the height of the counters."

Hannah grinned up at him. "I can see why that might be an issue." Heck, with a standard height counter or island, John Henry would have to spend his entire shift nearly bent in half just to work.

"Thought you might."

"Hey, Mike, toss me your tape measure," she called out, and snagged the heavy measure when it sailed across the room toward her.

"Nice catch."

"Thanks." She pulled on the tape measure, set one end on the floor and told John Henry, "The standard height for a kitchen counter is thirty-six inches. Hits most of us about at the hips."

"Not me," he said, laughing.

"True." She grinned. "For you, I was thinking we could make the counters about forty inches high and that should help you out a lot."

"It's great for me, but no one else in my crew is as vertically blessed as I am." Smiling, he said, "If you could do one of the prep counters at forty inches and leave the rest the standard, that would work."

She hadn't expected that and gave him a smile of approval. "Well, that's really nice of you to think of everyone else."

"There are a couple of my sous-chefs who might have to drag in a box to stand on if I had all the counters that high."

"I would sure need one," Hannah said, and found herself really relaxing and enjoying herself with the big man.

"You are a small one," he said, then he looked around again. "Another thing that's high on my list? A twelve-burner gas stove a couple inches taller than standard."

"I think we can handle that." In fact, she liked him so much, Hannah knew she'd turn everything upside down to find one if she had to.

She led him through the kitchen and back into the dining area. Sunlight streamed through the wide windows and construction dust danced in the beams.

"Is there anything else you need in there?"

He looked down at her and shook his head. "Not that I can think of right now. But if something comes to me, I'll let you know."

"Just call me," she said, and dug one of her business cards out of her back pocket. "My cell number's there, too."

"Thanks, I will." He gave another long look around, then said, "When I leave here, I'm charging all-new skillets and saucepans to Bennett. And whatever else I can find." He clapped his hands together and scrubbed his palms eagerly.

"Ben told me you were supposed to get whatever you wanted for the kitchen."

John Henry's eyebrows lifted. "Ben, is it?"

She frowned a little, embarrassed at the slip. "He's just so…stiff."

"Yeah, I suppose he is, mostly. But I run my kitchen my way and not many chefs can claim that, so I cut him some slack."

"Wish he'd let me run my job site my way," she muttered.

"If it helps," he said, glancing around the room again, "I think you're doing a great job. I can see how it's going to look and I'm impressed."

Hannah sighed and smiled. "I appreciate that. And if you wouldn't mind, maybe you could tell Bennett Carey that you think so."

He laughed, a loud, rolling thunder kind of sound that rippled through the work site. "Hell, Bennett knows damn well you're doing a good job. The man just cannot relax. He's always been that way. Got to stay on top of everything. Make sure everyone else is doing a job he thinks he could do better."

Now Hannah laughed because he was absolutely right. "You described King Carey perfectly."

"King Carey?" he repeated, and laughed again.

"Didn't mean to say that," she admitted. "It's just what I call him in my head."

"It fits," he said, nodding. "But Bennett is also the best friend I ever had. He's a man you can count on. And if he gives you his word, he'll die before he breaks it."

Hannah looked up into his deep brown eyes and saw understanding shining there. As if he knew she was having a really hard time dealing with his friend and he was trying to tell her to hang in there. "You really think a lot of him, don't you?"

"None higher," he said. "He's a good guy, Hannah. But I think you already know that."

Maybe she did, Hannah thought. The problem was, if she let herself believe it, then she might get drawn even deeper into the feelings for him that were already growing. She couldn't really risk that, given what she'd already lived through once in her life.

Because no matter what John Henry said, the truth was that Bennett Carey lived in a whole different world than she did and nothing good ever happened when worlds collided.

Bennett fought traffic all the way to LA and silently blamed Hannah for cursing him.

Hell, he blamed Hannah for ruining his whole damn day. Nothing had gone right, starting with the traffic. His first meeting had been a disaster—he'd walked out when the opposing CEO had refused to deal. The second one, with a Realtor trying to negotiate for her client on land she owned in Irvine, had fallen apart when Bennett saw the geologist's report.

Thanks to Hannah, his mind hadn't been on anything but her. Even meeting up with Amanda's fiancé, Henry, for lunch hadn't taken the edge off.

In fact, it had gotten worse. Henry and Bennett had once been great friends, until Amanda fell in love with Henry and Bennett had stumbled across the couple right after they'd had sex. What had followed was a short fistfight and a ten-year rivalry that had only ended recently.

"Damn it." Bennett stopped behind a delivery truck and put the BMW into Neutral. With traffic back to Orange County a typical nightmare, Bennett knew he'd be there for a while. He'd even stayed in LA later than he'd had to, hoping to miss most of the rush hour freeway mess. "For all the good that did me," he muttered.

While music pumped out around him, Bennett let his mind wander, and naturally, it went straight to that morning.

Hannah was driving him crazy. Not once in his life had he ever been attracted to a woman more at home in jeans than business wear or elegant dresses. She was tiny, but strong and so damn self-confident they kept butting heads. And damn it, he liked that, too. He'd never known a woman to argue with him like Hannah did. Or to challenge him. Or to call him out for scowling at her.

He shouldn't appreciate her so much, but he did, and now that he'd had a taste of her, he wanted more.

Traffic inched forward, and while he grumbled to himself about having to be in Los Angeles at all, Bennett thought about lunch with Henry.

At a busy, popular Mexican restaurant, Henry took a sip of his beer and said, "Amanda says you're trying to convince your mom to move out of your house."

"Trying and failing," Bennett admitted, and picked up his own beer. "Unless you and my sister are willing to take her in."

"I am, but Mandy says no way. She's convinced your mom will drive her nuts over the wedding planning." Henry shrugged. "I wouldn't mind at all. You know I always liked your mom and dad."

"I know."

"But hell, Bennett, Mandy's making me insane with wedding stuff already. If I had both of them doing it? No, thanks."

Bennett sighed and reluctantly admitted, "I get it." He didn't want to understand, but hell. He was on Henry's side in this, and that was unusual enough since he and his old friend had been at war for the last ten years. He was glad their friendship was finally getting back on track, though.

"How about you get Mandy to work on getting our father to come around?" he asked. "If she can't badger him into actual retirement, nothing can."

"*I should complain about you calling my fian-cée a nag,*" *Henry mused with a smile,* "*but since you're her brother and you've known her longer, I'll let it ride.*"

"*Thanks.*"

"*How's the reno on the restaurant coming?*"

And just like that, the tension was back and Ben-nett's heartbeat spiked. "*It's only been a week, but seems to be moving along.*"

"*That's it?*" *Henry just stared at him.* "*That's your whole report? Mandy says you're stopping in at The Carey every damn day to ride herd on your contractor, and all I get is 'it's coming along'?*"

"*Mandy's got a big mouth.*"

Henry winced. "*See, there you go again. I should be giving you a hard time over that one, too. But yeah, she does. So why are you stopping in every day? Don't trust your contractor?*"

Trust. *Well, that was a question. He was begin-ning to think she was as good at her job as she'd claimed to be. But what she was doing to him, he hadn't counted on. And didn't know what the hell to do about it.*

"*Ah,*" *Henry said thoughtfully,* "*so what's she like?*"

"*What?*"

"*The contractor. What's she like?*"

"*Annoying.*"

Henry laughed.

"Thanks very much. So happy you're amused."

"Oh, come on, Bennett. It's great for me, seeing a woman get under your skin."

"I didn't say that."

"Didn't have to, man. It's clear."

"The only thing that's clear," Bennett said, *"is that this conversation is over."*

Henry laughed outright, set his beer down and leaned toward him. *"Come on. You've got to see my side."*

"Your side of what?"

"Hell, Bennett. When Amanda was driving me nuts, can you really tell me you didn't enjoy every damn minute?"

No. He couldn't. He had relished Amanda giving Henry a hard time. But their situation had been different, Bennett assured himself. As much as she hadn't wanted to admit it, Amanda had loved Henry, so naturally, he thought, she'd tortured him.

There was no love between him and Hannah. There was plenty of heat, he could admit to that. And, he thought that maybe sex with her would probably burn out that flame and finally give him some peace of mind. Once he'd had her, he could stop thinking about her. Wondering what she would feel like under him. Over him.

He rubbed his forehead and stifled a groan.

"Yeah," Henry said as he sat back and lifted his

beer in a silent toast. "I'm enjoying the hell out of this."

When the car behind him in the chaotic mess of the 405 honked at him, Bennett jerked out of his memories and moved the three feet forward that traffic allowed him.

If he survived this trip, he was going straight to the restaurant. It was time he and Hannah had a long talk.

Hannah loved being alone on the site.

And today she needed it more than ever.

She'd let the crew go at six because they'd all been putting in a lot of overtime and she didn't want to wear them out when they still had so far to go. But as for her, having this time to herself, in the quiet, gave her a chance to unwind at her own pace. And since the kitchen was at the back of the restaurant, far from the street, it was as if she were alone in the world. Considering the day she'd had so far, alone was a very good thing.

She stood back to check out the work done so far. Under the glare of the bare, overhead lightbulbs, the kitchen looked like less of a disaster area and more like a work in progress. Without the crew there, she could concentrate on a few of the touches she thought would give the kitchen just a little extra oomph.

Hannah smiled to herself as she spread wood glue on a pine slat, then crouched to apply it to the end of a new cabinet. The slats were decorative, and when the cabinets were painted, the extra pieces would look as if they'd been carved into the cabinets themselves.

When she had the last slat in place, she reached down for the right-angle wood clamp. She had to clamp the wood overnight to give the glue a chance to set up.

Smiling to herself, Hannah kept her left hand on the slat and swept out to reach the clamp. And couldn't. "Damn it."

"What's wrong?"

She jolted and just managed to swallow a shout of surprise. Looking back over her shoulder, Hannah said, "What are you doing here, Ben?"

"I went by your house. You weren't there. So I came here."

"Because you assumed I had no life?"

"No because I assumed you'd be working overtime to earn that bonus."

"Okay," she allowed with a shrug, "good assumption."

"So I repeat. What's wrong?"

She blew out a breath. "I can't reach the wood clamp."

He walked closer, every step measured, as if he were crossing a minefield. And hell, maybe he was. After the way they'd left things that morning, not surprising that they were both a little… Defensive.

"This?" He bent down, scooped up the tool and held it out to her.

"Yes. And as long as you're here, you can put it on while I hold the slat in place."

"And how do I do that?"

She smiled up at him, surprised he was willing to admit there was something he couldn't do. Why did that make her like him just a little more?

"Open the mouth of the clamp and set it right here, against the corner of the cabinet. That way it holds the slat in place."

Frowning to himself, he concentrated on aligning the tool perfectly and when he had it right, she said, "Now tighten it. You don't have to go nuts, just tight enough to make sure it holds."

She watched him concentrate and realized that she wanted that focus on her. The KISS—she thought of it in capital letters—had haunted her all day. She hadn't wanted it to, but also hadn't been able to stop it. Hannah knew better. Knew she shouldn't be fantasizing about Bennett Carey, but thoughts about him gnawed at the edges of her mind constantly.

For days now, she'd felt a buzz of expectation humming throughout her body, and every night she tossed and turned through dreams where Bennett Carey was the master of all lovers. She really wanted to find out if her dreams were remotely close to reality.

"Is that good?" he asked.

"What?"

"The clamp," he said. "Is that good?"

"Oh. Yeah. Yeah, it's fine." She let go of the wooden slat and when Bennett stood up, she tested the clamp just to make sure.

"Had to check?" he asked.

She looked up at him. "Wouldn't you?"

He smiled. "Yes, I would."

Why did he have to smile? That one small expression, however brief, changed everything about him. His eyes got warmer, the tension dropped out of his shoulders and he became even more tempting than when he scowled at her.

With her head tipped back, she looked into his eyes—those clear lake-blue eyes that were so hard to read and so rarely shone with laughter. He was a mystery to her. A man who seemed so closed down, but who had such fire in those eyes. A man who could spark her temper in a blink and spark desire even faster.

Why was she so intrigued by a man she shouldn't even be looking at?

God, it was so quiet in the kitchen, she could hear her own heartbeat thundering in her ears. How had she gotten to this point? From the first, he'd attracted her. Then, in spite of his crabby attitude, she'd liked him. The heat between them had always been there, and now it burned so fiercely she could hardly remember a time when she *didn't* want Ben with a need that was soul deep.

Was this more than like? Probably. Most likely. Oh, she didn't want to take that last, long tumble into love, because she just couldn't risk it again. Risk loving a rich man only for him to turn on her. She had to find a way to stop the slippery slide toward loving Ben because they would never be together. His world and hers were too far apart.

But that simple truth didn't seem to be enough to keep her from caring, more and more. How could one week change so much without really changing anything?

"So," she asked, when she was sure her voice wouldn't quiver, "why did you come looking for me?"

His gaze locked on hers. "I thought we should… talk about this morning."

"What is there to talk about?" *So much*, she thought.

He moved in closer, and it was only then she noticed that he'd taken his tie off and the collar of his shirt was opened. Hell, that was practically naked for Bennett Carey.

Naked.

She shook her head hoping to clear it but all she accomplished was making herself a little dizzier than she already was. Probably not good.

"You said you kissed me because I needed it."

"And you kissed me back for the same reason?"

"More or less," he admitted, then moved in even closer until she could see the tension in his eyes and feel heat pumping from his body. "So tell me, Hannah. What do I need now?"

Her mouth went dry. His eyes told her exactly what he needed. And in this particular area, they were just alike.

"Look," she said, trying and failing to smooth out the situation, "I just thought we should get that kiss out of the way because it just felt like it was *there*, all the time. You know, building sexual tension and—"

"Uh-huh," he said. "So it wasn't just need. It was clearing the air."

"Exactly!" Pleased, she nodded and gave him a smile that felt a little shaky. Because that kiss hadn't cleared up anything. It had clouded the situation even more than it had been, and right now, she felt as if she were completely blind.

"Right." He was so close now she could see the pulse beat at the base of his throat. It was fast. Like hers.

Hannah realized that by kissing Ben that morning, she'd started something that couldn't be stopped. The silence in the restaurant was overpowering and in the strained quiet, the only sounds she heard were her own heartbeat and the rush of her own breath.

"Ben," she whispered, her gaze locked on his, "this isn't a good idea."

"No?" He shook his head, never taking his eyes off her. "You're wrong, Hannah. It's the only idea that matters at the moment."

She swallowed hard and waited. For what, she wasn't entirely sure. But in the next moment, Ben cleared that up for her.

"We should probably get something else out of the way, don't you think?" In a finger snap, he snaked his arms out and pulled her in close, then bent to take her mouth with a hunger that matched her own.

Hannah simply dissolved for one long, luscious moment. Her head spun crazily, and everything in her kindled in the fires he was stoking. Her breath was gone and she didn't care if it came back. She clutched at his shoulders to hold herself up. Their tongues tangled in a wild, frenzied dance of lust that clanged in her head like alarm bells. But it was too late for internal warnings. She'd had her chance to keep her distance and instead had allowed herself to feel…too much for a man she shouldn't have allowed into her heart in the first place.

His hands stroked up and down her back with a fierce possessiveness that pulsated inside her. Hannah gave herself up to it, exploring his mouth with the same intensity he gave her. It was as if every moment spent with him, every bit of sexual tension and heat had suddenly burst through a closed and locked door to demand satisfaction.

When he abruptly broke the kiss and looked down

at her, Hannah had to blink a few times, just to bring him into focus. Breath raging, heart near to bursting, she looked up into those deep blue eyes as he asked, "So is it out of the way yet?"

A harsh, broken laugh shot from her throat. "You know, I think we still have work to do."

His lips twitched. "I'm your man."

For now, she thought, then stopped thinking entirely. When he kissed her again it was as if he'd slipped a leash that had been holding him back as she had been restraining herself.

The calm, rational Bennett Carey disappeared and Ben—a man with no control, no boundaries stepped in to take over. His hands were everywhere. She felt him as if he were surrounding her. His breath brushed against her skin. His lips trailed up and down her throat, and his hands moved over her, exploring what felt like every inch of her. He touched her face, her throat, skimmed one hand down her shirt, and even through the fabric and her bra, her breast burned when he touched her.

Her head fell back as he held her tighter, tighter. His mouth took hers and then slid from her lips to the length of her throat, licking, tasting, nibbling until she was one raw nerve. Her heart pounded so hard, she was surprised it didn't simply jump right out of her chest. Her whole body felt as if it was on a high burn, and every time he touched her, kissed her, it only increased the heat.

"Oh, Ben…" Words slipped past the knot in her throat, and she caught her breath on the last one.

"No more talking," he muttered. "We don't need words now."

He undid the button and zipper on her jeans and slid one hand down and under the slender elastic of her panties to touch her. Cup her. His mouth took hers again as she rocked into his touch and groaned aloud at the first stroke of his fingers.

It had been so long since she'd been touched. Since she'd felt a man's need for her. Since she'd shared that need, and Hannah wasn't about to waste a second wondering if they were doing the right thing or not.

He tore his hand free, broke their kiss and looked wild as he stared down at her. His eyes flashed with desire, with need, with the same fires now engulfing Hannah.

"That's it," he muttered. "Now. It's got to be now, so if you're going to change your mind, here's your chance."

Changing her mind wasn't even an option. All Hannah wanted now was to be with him. To take all he offered and give him what they both wanted so badly. Decisions had been made. Steps taken. Everything she had ever done had brought her to this moment, and she didn't want to be anywhere else.

She looked up into those lake-blue eyes with fires kindled deep inside them, and said, "You're wasting time."

Eight

He laughed. A short, sharp bark of amusement that both fed the fire engulfing her and made her grin in response. "I like that about you, Hannah. I never have to guess what you're thinking."

She reached up and cupped his cheek in her palm. Instantly, his smile faded and desire swamped his features again. This Ben Carey was one she hardly recognized. But she liked him. A lot.

In one smooth move, he lifted her off her feet and Hannah instinctively wrapped her legs around his waist. It felt so good to be pressed tightly to him. His arms were like a vise around her and she loved it. His breathing was harsh, strained and she understood. She felt his heartbeat hammering in rhythm to her own. And she wriggled against the hard length of him pressing into her body.

He carried her to the nearest wall and she grinned when he slammed her back against it and instantly began undoing her jeans and pulling them down. She twisted and writhed in his arms, helping as much as she could without him putting her down. Clearly he had no intention of letting her go. He held her pinned against the wall and reached down to pull off one of her boots and one leg of her jeans.

"Hurry," Hannah whispered on a choked laugh.

"I am," he insisted, and straightened to kiss her again. "The jeans look great on you, but a skirt would have been easier."

"Not to work in," she said, and caught his face in her hands to kiss him with everything she had. He groaned and snapped the band of her black bikini underwear.

Pulling her mouth from his, Hannah laughed wildly, and then she reached for his slacks and in a few seconds, she had him free and curled her fingers around him.

Bennett groaned harder, deeper when she touched him, and she watched him grit his teeth as if he were calling on every ounce of control he possessed. Hannah knew how he felt because she was so desperate for him, so incredibly beyond ready, she felt as if she might explode before they actually got down to doing the deed.

"You should know," she managed to say, "I don't normally do things like this."

"Neither do I. Don't care."

"Yeah, but just wanted you to know."

"Consider me informed," he said, and buried his face in the curve of her neck.

"Ohhh…" she said on a moan, while he ran his tongue over her pulse beat "…you should hurry."

"That's the plan," he muttered against her throat.

And then he was there, driving into her heat, and Hannah stopped thinking entirely. Nothing mattered but what he was doing to her. What he was making her feel. Hannah held on and moved with him, taking him deeper, higher. At the small of his back, she dug her heels in, pulling him to her, holding him close. Closer.

"Ben! Ben…" Her head fell back against the wall, and she fought for breath as he continued to claim her body with a single-minded concentration that pushed her ever nearer to the edge of a release that threatened to shake her to her soul.

"Damn it, Hannah," he ground out, "just let go. Let go and fall."

She wanted to, and at the same time, she wanted to hold out against a climax and simply revel in the ride. But her body wouldn't allow her to wait. The coils of tension within tightened until it was desperation that drove her.

"Close. So. Close." She lifted her head, looked into his eyes and saw the same desperation she was feeling reflected back at her.

In the next moment, the world tilted, and all she could see were the fireworks shattering behind her eyes. Her body tightened, coiled, then burst with an orgasm that stopped her world. She'd expected, hoped for a "pop" of release because it had been a long time since she'd been with a man. But Ben Carey's skills—even up against a wall—were so incredible that she was trembling and holding on to him just so she wouldn't slide off the face of the Earth. She cried out his name and clutched at his shoulders with a desperate grip as her body rocked on and on.

And moments later, she held him as he fought through that last barrier and claimed what he'd already given her. Her world tilted wildly and then steadied again as her heart thudded in her chest. What swept through her was a warmth she'd never known. A *connection* to this man she'd known for only a week.

She didn't question it because what would have been the point? It had happened. She'd taken that last, tumbling step into love, whether she wanted to or not. Brushing his hair with her fingers, she held his head against her and for just a moment, reveled in what she was feeling.

Dangerous, she told herself, but the warning was too late, and if it had come earlier, she didn't know that she would have listened anyway. His strength wrapped around her. His breath dusted against her skin and his galloping heartbeat slammed in time with her own.

So unexpected. So… Scary. And yet, somehow wonderful.

When they could both breathe again, he lifted his head, looked at her and said, "Hi."

She laughed and held him tighter. She might love him, but she also knew enough to know he wouldn't want to hear that, so she said, "Yeah, hi to you, too. That was…"

"Surprising," he finished for her.

"Yeah. Good word." She didn't want to move but knew she had to. When he shifted to set her on her feet, Hannah braced her back against the wall again, this time for balance.

"Stupid time to bring this up," Ben said as they both rearranged their clothes. And Hannah bent to scoop up her discarded boot and put it back on.

"I wasn't thinking," he blurted out as if he couldn't believe that himself. "And I haven't carried condoms with me since I was eighteen hoping to get lucky."

She looked up at him. "Well, we're covered as long as you're healthy."

"I am." He looked insulted that she would think otherwise.

"Me, too. I'm also on birth control, so not a problem."

He pushed both hands through his hair, walked a few steps away, then swung around and came back to her. "Well, it's a problem for me."

And in a blink, she thought with an inner sigh, Ben was gone and Bennett was back.

"Didn't seem to be an issue for you a minute ago," she pointed out.

"True. But I don't treat women like this. Slamming you up against a wall—"

"It's a good wall. And trust me," she added, "I didn't mind a bit."

He laughed shortly and scrubbed one hand across the back of his neck. "I shouldn't have…"

"*You* didn't do anything. *We* did," she said, "and if you're going to have regrets and start beating yourself up over this, you should know I don't want to hear it." How could she not love him? she asked herself. So ready to berate himself for something she too had clearly wanted.

"You don't have regrets?"

"I try not to," she said. "About anything." Frowning slightly, she muttered, "Doesn't always work."

"Nice if you can do it."

"It takes practice." She looked at him and saw that he was thinking and rethinking what had just happened, and Hannah tried not to take it personally. For Bennett Carey, having a woman against a wall in an empty restaurant was probably so shocking he didn't know what to do next.

Well, she did.

"You know what?" Walking up to him, she laid one hand on his chest and smiled to herself when he lifted one hand to cover hers. "This was a first for me, too."

"Great. That makes me feel better." He was scowling again and for some odd reason, Hannah found it…endearing. He was clearly so far out of his comfort zone, he was off-balance. But then, so was she. It wasn't every day you discovered you were in love with a man you never should have gotten involved with. A contrary man who loved schedules and rarely laughed. A rich man who could, if he wanted to, ruin her. A man she'd known about ten minutes.

But time, it seemed, had nothing to do with what she felt. And she knew that he wouldn't want to hear it. Heck, she wasn't ready to *feel* it.

"If it helps, I feel great."

He laughed and her breath caught. Bennett Carey was gorgeous when he was scowling, but when the man really smiled, it was heart-stopping. Was it any wonder she'd been toast right from the beginning?

Hannah went up on her toes and brushed her lips against his. "I think we could both use a glass of wine and something to eat."

He looked into her eyes and nodded. "Among other things."

She blew out a breath. "You remember where I live, right?"

"I do."

"Then let's lock up and go see what's in my freezer."

When she started walking, Bennett's hand came down on her shoulder and he spun her around to face him. Staring into her eyes, he said, "I don't know what the hell's happening here, Hannah. This wasn't the plan."

"Not everything has to be planned, Ben."

His lips curved briefly, but he shook his head. "In my world, they do."

"You're in my world now," she pointed out with a smile.

"True," he said with a quick glance at the work-in-progress job site surrounding them. "So I guess you should know. I'm not finished with you yet."

"Me, either," she said, and since she did know what was happening—at least with her—she reached up to smooth his hair back from his forehead. "That's why we need the meal."

Bennett waited while she tore open a frozen pizza and watched as she turned the oven on to preheat it. Her kitchen was small. Hell, the whole house could have fit inside his home three or four times. The walls were a lemon yellow and the cabinets were dark green. And even while he noticed, he silently admitted that he didn't give a good damn what color her kitchen was.

Instead, he focused on her. That short, black hair of hers he now knew was as smooth as silk. Her compact, curvy body fit against him as if she were a missing piece, locking into place.

That thought brought him up short. He wasn't looking for missing pieces. He was only trying to get her out of his system, not deeper into it. That's why he was here, he assured himself. To burn out this… Whatever it was between them. Once that was done, things could get back to normal.

She turned her head to look at him, and when she smiled, everything inside him fisted. He was hard and hot and aching for her and damned if he wanted to wait for a frozen pizza. He pushed off the wall, crossed the small room and picked her up.

Laughing, she asked, "What are you doing?"

"Looking for a bedroom," he muttered past the knot of need in his throat. "Any bedroom."

She hooked her arms around his neck and said, "Down the hall, first door on the left."

It didn't take long to make the trip. And he didn't care. All he could think about now, was the small, strong woman wrapped around him. Her humor, her strength and the way she tasted and smelled, crawled into his system and crowded out every other thought. In her room, he didn't bother to look at the surroundings. All he needed was a horizontal surface, and if she didn't have a bed, the floor would have to do.

"Thank God," he muttered, "a bed."

"Well, of course there's a bed," she said, still laughing.

He'd never known a woman like her. No other woman he'd ever been with would laugh during sex. Always before, sex had been quietly satisfying. Civilized. But Hannah Yates had changed everything. She was changing *him*. He was different with her than he was with anyone else. He knew it. What he *didn't* know was how he felt about that. At the moment though, all he cared about was her. Being with Hannah again. Watching her eyes glaze over with pleasure. Feeling her hands on him.

Bennett dropped her on the bed and tore at his clothes, while he watched her do the same. He couldn't remember a single time in his life when he'd been as eager for anything as he was to be able to indulge himself—and her, as they hadn't taken the time to do at the restaurant. Moonlight pooled in the room and draped across her now naked body like silk. And when she smiled at him, all thoughts vanished from his mind.

He covered her body with his and took the moment to relish the feel of her soft skin against his. She sighed and he felt it deep inside him. Bennett didn't want to think about what that meant, so he shut his mind down and instead focused only on touching her. He couldn't get enough of her. So small, so strong, so soft. She was, at the moment, *everything*.

"I've been wanting this for days," he whispered.

"Me, too," she said, and trailed one finger down the center of his chest, making him shiver.

"It'll be better than the wall."

"I don't know," she said, scraping her fingers along his back. "The wall was pretty impressive."

"I do my best work horizontal."

"Guess you're going to have to prove that," she said, and arched into him.

"I love a challenge," he whispered, and kissed her, diving into her mouth, her breath, her sighs.

Then he drew back, cupped her breasts in his palms and reveled in the way she reacted, tipping her head back, closing her eyes and arching into his touch. She was so expressive, holding nothing back, and that made him want to give her more. Sliding along her body, he swept one hand down the length of her while once again claiming her mouth, that amazing mouth, with his. She threaded her fingers through his hair and parted her lips for him. Their tongues tangled in a breathless dance that pushed them both along a now familiar road to an ending that he already knew would be shattering.

She shifted slightly to run her hands up and down his back, and her calloused, gentle touch drove him crazy. Minutes that could have been hours passed and he couldn't wait a moment longer. He slipped into her heat in a long, slow slide that had her moaning and his own self-control dissolving.

Her legs came up and around his hips, and when he moved, she moved with him, creating a friction of desire that pushed them both.

"You feel so good, Hannah," he ground out, looking down into her green eyes that seemed to hold the world's secrets.

"Ben...you make me feel..." Her voice broke off on a sigh, and he wished he knew what she was going to say. He wanted all of her and that want was startling to him. He'd wanted to burn her out of his system, and instead, he had the distinct impression now that he was burning her into his very bones.

But that was a worry for another day.

Tonight, there was only now.

She sighed his name as her body tightened around his, and Bennett pushed her harder, drove them both a little crazier with a faster pace that she raced to match. Suddenly, Hannah caught his face in her hands drew his head down to hers and kissed him as her body shook and trembled with an orgasm that was so rich and full, he felt it, as well.

And while she kissed him, he let himself join her in the fall.

"Where is Bennett?" Serena looked around the Carey Center as if half expecting her older brother to pop up from behind a row of seats.

"I don't know," Amanda said. "This is not like Bennett. He's *late*."

Jack Colton and Henry Porter sat behind their fiancés and shared a knowing look.

"Perhaps," Candace Carey said as she lifted Alli onto her lap, "Bennett has finally decided that having a life is more important than sacrificing yourself on the Carey Corporation altar."

"Candy," Martin said, sparing a quick glance at his daughters. "I'm here, aren't I?"

She turned to spear him with a glare. "Being at the last auditions for the Summer Stars program is *not* getting a life. It's a part of our business."

"I can't win with you," he muttered.

"Of course you can," Candace said, giving Alli a hug. "You just don't like what you have to do to win."

Martin slumped back in his chair and glowered silently.

When the next contestant walked across the stage, looking nervous, Serena leaned into Amanda. "Should we call Bennett? Make sure he's okay?"

Henry's muffled laughter had both women turning to look at him. Shaking his head, Henry said, "I saw him earlier today, and if I'm right…Bennett's more than fine and you really don't want to call him."

"Damn it!" Bennett jolted up in bed, and Hannah's head slid off his chest to land on the mattress.

"Hey!" So much for the cozy afterglow. "What's wrong?"

He turned to look at her. "Sorry. Sorry."

She felt her heart do a long, slow and probably inevitable roll. His hair was tousled, his eyes shadowed and oh, that talented mouth of his was, once again, scowling. "What're you doing?"

"I'm supposed to be at the Carey Center right now." He glanced at his watch as if to confirm what he already knew.

Hannah laughed. "Even naked, you check your watch?"

"I'm *late*."

He said those two words as if they were a particularly complicated foreign language. Shaking her head, Hannah sat up, rubbed one hand across his shoulders, because she needed to touch him again, then teased, "But you're *never* late."

He whipped his head around to give her an even deeper scowl, and Hannah laughed harder.

"I'm glad you're enjoying yourself," he muttered. What the hell was happening to him? So wrapped up in a woman he forgot his obligations? First time he'd experienced *that*. But then, everything about Hannah was a new experience, wasn't it?

"Very much," she said, grinning. "So. Your choices are, to get dressed and race to the Center. *Or*, stay here and have a naked pizza picnic in my bed, followed by…*dessert*."

One corner of his mouth tipped up as he stared at her. She was intoxicating. His sexy pixie. The last thing he wanted to do right then was leave. His body was already stirring for her again, and he vaguely wondered if he would *ever* be able to get enough of her. Everything was changing, and he wasn't sure how he felt about it. But now didn't seem the time for self-reflection.

"Well?" she asked, running one hand through that short, spiky hair.

Very deliberately, he undid the clasp on his watch and tossed it over his shoulder to land on his discarded suit. "It's been a long time since I was on a picnic."

"Oh, I love a good picnic." She held his face in her hands and kissed him until he laid her down on the bed again.

Pizza came much later.

At the Center the following day, Bennett managed to avoid answering questions from his family. Not showing up where he was supposed to be was so out of character for him, it was no wonder they were curious. But he wasn't about to satisfy that curiosity. Hell, he couldn't explain it to himself.

He'd finally left Hannah's house about 2:00 a.m. and, on that long drive back to his place in Dana Point, had a singularly futile argument with himself. Being with Hannah had affected him more than he had thought it would. She was impossibly attractive, amused at all the wrong times and strong enough that when he said he had to leave, she'd kissed him goodbye and watched him go without trying to convince him to stay.

Why hadn't she wanted him to stay?

"Damn woman is confusing the hell out of me." Shutting her out of his mind, he turned to the sheaf of papers on his desk and tried to concentrate on work. If a sexy pixie slipped past those mental barriers now and then, it wasn't because he hadn't tried.

He was grateful when his office door swung open. Until he saw his father. Then he figured an argument with someone besides himself might be more satisfying.

"Hi, Dad. What's up?"

"What's *up*?" Martin stalked across the room and dropped into one of the visitor chairs opposite Bennett's desk. "Your mother has a lunch date. With a *man.*"

"Really?" Surprise colored his tone, and he had to wonder what his mother was up to. She'd moved into his house to bring his father around and that obviously wasn't working. Had she moved on to a more devious plan?

Women really were dangerous.

"Of course really. Why would I say it if I didn't mean it?"

"You wouldn't."

"Exactly." Martin jumped up from the chair as if he were on a spring. Walking in a tight circle, Martin waved both hands in the air. "It's Evan Williams."

Bennett frowned to himself. "You mean the manager for the San Diego chorus?"

Martin jabbed his finger at his son. "That's the one."

"But isn't he around forty?"

His father stopped in a slice of sunlight that worked to define the misery on the man's face and the powerless sheen in his eyes. Martin Carey was worried. About time, too, Bennett told himself.

"Thirty-eight," Martin snapped. "That rat bastard is thirty-eight! What the hell is your mother thinking? A younger man? Why is she doing this?"

Bennett smothered a smile he hadn't expected.

"Hell," Martin continued, "why is *he* doing this?"

"Mom's a beautiful woman," Bennett said thoughtfully.

Martin's gaze snapped to his son, irritation carved into his features. "Well, I know that."

"Have you told her that lately?"

"She has a mirror, doesn't she?"

Bennett's eyes rolled. "Dad—"

"I know, I know." He waved one hand. "Stupid thing to say."

"Or think."

"That, too. But damn it, she's my *wife*. She's moved out of our house. She's got a *date*, for God's sake, with a man young enough to be her son…" He walked over and dropped into the chair again. "And she won't talk to me."

"Because it doesn't do her any good," Bennett said, and realized that something had shifted for him. He'd tried very hard not to get involved in the Retirement Wars, but now, he could see exactly what his mother had been talking about.

Bennett had wanted his father to retire because, by God, *he* was the CEO now. It was his turn to run the family company. To build on it just as Martin had. Now, though, he could see that Martin had spent so many years devoted to the company that he'd actually *forgotten* how to have a life, too.

Last night had brought that home to Bennett. He prided himself on timeliness. On being where he was supposed to be at all times. A schedule kept the world from spinning out of control.

And yet, a night with Hannah had shown him that tossing that schedule aside could open you up to all kinds of interesting possibilities. Maybe keeping a daily list of obligations, responsibilities and duties wasn't the key to happiness. Maybe he didn't actually need to wear his watch every day of his life. Maybe he needed to embrace the kind of freedom Hannah represented.

Even as that thought settled in his mind, he mentally reeled back from it. Was he really trying to rethink his entire world after knowing this woman for little more than a week? Preposterous. He liked his life just as it was. Hannah was an intriguing… Aberration. They didn't have a relationship. What they had was great sex and a business deal.

"Are you listening to me?" his father demanded, drawing Bennett out of his thoughts.

"Not really," he admitted. "Dad, nothing's changed. Mom's going to lunch with a man who wants to spend time with her. I don't blame her."

"Whose side are you on?"

"Mine," Bennett murmured, then louder, he said, "If you want Mom back, then pay attention to her. Stop complaining and take care of it."

"My own son." Martin rose slowly and gave Bennett a hard look. "I come to you for help and this is what I get? Complaining, is it? You think any of this is easy? It's not. Just you wait until you've got a woman tying your guts into knots. Then we'll see how much complaining *you* do."

"Which is why," Bennett said softly as his father stormed from the office, "I will never let a woman tie my guts into knots."

"This is just…delicious." Amanda Carey nudged her sister, Serena, and both women laughed and leaned in closer to Hannah. "He missed an appointment," Amanda said, clearly delighted. "That never happens, Hannah. And, since you are the only new player in Bennett's oh-so-organized world, we figured that you're behind that particular miracle. So we had to come and meet you!"

"Exactly," Serena said, reaching out to give Hannah's hand a pat. "We had to see the woman who's managed to throw Bennett's world out of alignment."

Hannah was still a little stunned by the visit. Ben's sisters had shown up at the job site and insisted on taking her off for lunch so they could "chat." That had thrown her off completely, but the Carey women would not be told no, and then Hank Yates had stepped in and told Hannah to go.

So here they were at a Mexican restaurant on Pacific Coast Highway, and Hannah could only listen as the sisters talked to and around her. Amanda had shoulder-length blond hair, blue eyes a little paler than Ben's and a square cut sapphire with a circle of diamonds glittering on her left ring finger.

Serena's hair was a little shorter, a little darker blond, and her blue eyes were darker than her sister's but lighter than Ben's. Her left ring finger boasted a gigantic emerald.

"Ben's world is still scheduled tightly. I haven't done anything," Hannah said, and took a sip of her iced tea.

"Ben?" Amanda grinned, and said, "No one has ever called him Ben. But you do. How interesting…"

"It's not—"

"I think he really likes you," Serena said softly.

"He's never just blown off an appointment before. Especially not one with the family."

"She's right," Amanda agreed. "He really does like you."

He wanted her—that much Hannah knew. But anything more than that? She didn't think so. Although, she remembered him tossing his watch over his shoulder. Maybe he liked her a little. Which was a pale emotion compared to the love she felt for him. "Oh? Did he tell you that?"

"Oh hell, no," Amanda said with a short laugh. "He'd rather have his tongue cut out."

"Charming, Mandy. Way to scare her off."

"She doesn't look like she scares easy," Amanda said.

"I don't." Hannah looked from one to the other of them. She really didn't know what to make of this meeting. She was an only child and had no idea how to deal with siblings. Anyone's siblings. "Look, I get you're his sisters and you're worried about him."

"No, that's not it at all," Amanda said, smiling. "Bennett can take care of himself. Usually. But not showing up last night? That's huge. That means something."

"We were…busy," Hannah said, and wished the waitress would show up with her tacos so she'd have something to stuff in her mouth.

"Well, that sounds interesting."

"Mandy…" Serena smiled at Hannah. "We really

only wanted to meet you. We're not trying to insinu-ate anything or embarrass you."

"I didn't—" Amanda cut herself off and shrugged. "She's right. I wasn't trying to give you a hard time. It's just that Bennett has always been such a man of routine—even when he was a kid—that we just had to meet the woman who could make him miss an appointment."

Hannah smiled at both of the women. She under-stood what they meant, and she appreciated it even though she didn't actually know what to do with it. "Look. It's really great of you both to come out to meet me. And I get why you wanted to. But there's nothing between Ben and me." Sadly, the only thing they shared was a night of amazing sex. She wasn't even sure they'd be repeating *that*, let alone share anything else.

Serena shook her head. "None of us believe that, Hannah. Not even you."

She sighed and turned her head to look out the window at the traffic passing on PCH. Laguna Beach was an arts and crafts kind of town, with more art galleries than restaurants. People flocked here for the spectacular scenery, the gorgeous beaches and the tide pools that had captivated generations of children. And right now, she wished she were outside, just one of the pedestrians wandering along the sidewalks.

It would be nice if she could believe Ben's sisters. Believe that he had feelings for her. But she couldn't.

Couldn't allow herself to believe it. Because even if he did care for her, what would it change? Yes, she loved him, but was love enough to bridge the differences between them?

"Even if I thought there could be, I wouldn't be interested."

"Well, why the hell not?" Amanda asked. "What's wrong with Ben—Bennett?"

"Nothing." She smiled because she admired loyalty and she loved that Bennett's sisters would come here to meet her, to defend him. "But we're from two different worlds and I've both been there and done that and have zero interest in doing it again."

"You make this sound like *West Side Story*," Serena said. "Or the Montagues and Capulets."

Hannah laughed a little as the waitress finally arrived with their lunches. She waited until the woman was gone again before saying, "Nothing quite so dramatic. But experience is a really good teacher." She took a breath and blew it out before she confessed, "I dated a rich guy once. I was even engaged to him. Briefly"

And never, she admitted silently, felt for him what she felt for Ben. How could she feel so much for him in so little time? Was it possible to love so quickly? And what was she supposed to do about it?

"Names," Amanda said, waving her fork. "I need names."

Hannah smiled and shrugged. What did it matter? "Davis Buckley."

"Oh." Serena's mouth twisted into a show of distaste. "Really, Hannah? Why on earth would you… no. Never mind." She held up a hand, backing off and admitting it was none of her business.

"Please, I'm not afraid to say it," Amanda spoke up. "The man is a toad, Hannah. What on earth did you see in him?"

Now that her tacos were there, she was ignoring her lunch completely. Thinking back, she could see how she'd been romanced into believing Davis's lies. Letting herself be blinded by the beautiful places he took her to, by the gifts he showered on her. By the empty words he offered her, promising to always be there for her. To give her the love she'd always dreamed of. But how to explain that to someone else?

"It was a combination of things, I guess," she finally said, and poked at her rice and beans with the tines of her fork. She could talk about it, though she hated remembering how stupid and trusting she'd been. "I'm embarrassed to say, Davis romanced me with flowers and attention and pretty words. My Dad was sick at the time, and I was lost and overwhelmed with the business, and Davis offered to help me with all of it.

"I believed I could trust him and I was wrong."

"Not surprising. Davis is very good at misrepresenting himself. And don't be embarrassed. We've all made blunders with men."

"Oh, have we ever," Serena murmured.

Hannah really appreciated the solidarity from Ben's sisters. She'd never had a lot of time in her life to make and keep good female friends. And sitting here across from these two women, Hannah realized how much she had missed by not having friends to talk with.

"Well, when he asked me to marry him, he swore he would help with the construction company because he believed in me." She looked at the other women and felt their sympathy before she added, "Instead of helping me though, he was trying to force me to quit the business and sell out.

"I finally discovered that he'd invested in a construction company that was in direct competition with us. So basically, if he could get me to leave Yates Construction, it was paving the way for his own new start-up."

"Devious man," Serena murmured.

Amanda nodded. "Like I said. A toad."

"Definitely toad-like," Hannah agreed. "When I broke off the engagement, he handed me a list of the money I owed him for his 'investment' in me."

"He hit a new low," Amanda said.

"I've almost paid him off, though it's taken me a long time. But when Ben offered us a bonus for finishing the restaurant in four weeks, I saw it as a gift from the construction gods. I can pay Davis off and get him out of my life forever."

There was a long moment of silence before Serena spoke up and said, "I admire you so much."

"Really, why?" Hannah turned to face the woman.

"Because you've made your own way. You built your company. You made a mistake, sure, but you're digging yourself out of it. That takes strength. I admire that," Serena said.

"So do I," Amanda added. "You didn't let the toad destroy you. And you're going to finish the restaurant job on time, so you'll have the bonus money to get rid of him forever. You're taking care of business. And that's excellent.

"Plus, you're getting to Bennett and that practically makes you a superhero!"

Hannah smiled, but she didn't know that Amanda was right about that. Oh, they were right about Davis. He was loathsome. But Ben was far wealthier than Davis Buckley, and that made her nervous. If Ben turned out to be as toady as Davis, he could ruin her business—or worse, pick up her debts and take it over. Okay, that sounded a little paranoid even to her. But who could blame her for being nervous after Davis?

She shook her head and took a bite of her taco. Silence stretched out for another minute or two, before Amanda spoke up again.

"It pains me to say this about my brother, who

at times makes me want to tear his hair out," she said, "but Bennett is nothing like Davis. *No one* is like Davis."

"True," Serena agreed.

"I get that," Hannah said. "But I don't want you guys to get the wrong idea. Whatever is going on between Ben and I isn't going to last. So there's no point in pretending it will. We're too different."

"You're both very hardheaded," Serena said. "So you have that in common."

"Good point," Amanda said, smiling at her sister.

"Funny." Hannah grinned. This lunch had turned out better than she'd thought it would. She'd enjoyed herself with the two women and had to wonder why they were so different from Bennett. Had he made a deliberate effort to be schedule driven and emotionally cut off? Why? Because he was the head of the Carey Corporation? Or had he simply gotten into the habit of keeping himself one step removed and only needed someone to push him out of that too-tight rut?

"You know," she mused, "Ben's really lucky to have you both."

Amanda reached out and gave her hand a squeeze. "Oh, be sure to tell him that, will you?"

Nine

Bennett walked into his house and was instantly assailed by an overly sweet, completely overpowering scent. Not surprising, he thought as he walked farther into what his family called the beige house.

Vases of roses were everywhere. Roses in full bloom. Rosebuds. Tiny roses. Even a damn rosebush in a huge clay pot! In every color of the rainbow, they were freaking everywhere. Walking through the foyer into the main room, Bennett looked around, stunned at the madness. On tables, along the hearth, on the floor, on the bay window.

Yet, past the roses, he took a look at his house and maybe for the first time, realized that his sisters and his mother might be right. His house—not a home, just a house—was as beige as his sisters had claimed. The furniture was spare and modern and looked as comfortable as a medieval rack. On the beige walls were white canvases with black spots and swirls that looked, he realized, like someone had turned his little niece loose with a paintbrush.

How had he never noticed this before? Because, he told himself, he was hardly ever here. When he was, he went straight to his bedroom. He didn't spend time in any of these rooms. He'd bought the house because it was a good investment. Because a man should own a house. Because… Hell, did it matter?

Instantly, an image of a tiny, lemon yellow kitchen leaped into his mind, and he quickly pushed it back out. This wasn't about Hannah. Not everything was about Hannah.

"Ah, Bennett!"

He closed his eyes briefly, then nodded. "Hello, Mother. I see Dad's sent you flowers."

She glanced around, then checked her hair in a mirror. "Yes. Another empty gesture."

His eyebrows lifted. "Several hundred roses is quite the gesture."

His mother just looked at him. "If it changes nothing," she said, "it means nothing."

How did he land in the middle of his parents' war?

"Mom," Bennett said quietly, "he's trying."

She looked up at him then, and he felt a swell

of love for the woman who'd always been the rock in their family. He hated seeing his parents at odds like this, but there didn't seem to be a damn thing he could do about helping the situation.

"I love your father, Bennett. But until he makes good on his promise, he's not really trying at all." She picked up a black leather bag and slipped it over her shoulder.

"Are you going out?" he asked, and noticed for the first time that she was wearing a cool blue dress and black heels.

"I am. I'm going to dinner. With Evan."

"I thought you had lunch with him." Bennett felt a quick blast of panic and instantly knew how his dad had felt earlier.

"I did. Now we're having dinner." She walked to the door. "He's a lovely man and I enjoy his company."

He thought about jumping in front of the door to block her escape but knew that wouldn't work. "Mom, he's only a few years older than *me*."

"Age doesn't mean anything, honey." She reached up and patted his cheek.

"Sure. And size doesn't matter."

She chuckled and shook her head. "Oh, don't look so horrified. I'm not doing anything wrong."

"You're married to my father and you're going on a date," he pointed out with what he considered remarkable patience.

"You're being silly, Bennett, and I just don't have time to listen right now." She walked to the door and stopped again. "Oh, before I forget. Amanda and Serena met your lady friend and liked her very much. I'm looking forward to meeting her myself."

A sinking sensation opened in his chest. "My what?"

"The woman you're seeing? I'm so happy you listened to me about having a healthy sexual relationship." She cocked her head to one side and studied him. "Honestly, Bennett, sweetheart. You must not have had sex yet because you still seem very tense. Maybe you should call that nice young woman the girls told me about and see if the two of you could have sex tonight."

He opened his mouth to say… *Something.* But nothing came out. What could he possibly say to that?

"Don't. Just…don't." What the hell was happening to his life? Lady friend? Sexual relationship? His *sisters*?

"Oh fine, Bennett. Won't say another word. But you should bring her to dinner." She leaned in and kissed his cheek. "Well, I have to rush. Don't wait up, sweetie."

And she was gone. *Don't wait up?* His mother was on a date. His sisters liked Hannah. *Bring her to dinner.* What the hell.

"No," he said aloud to the empty room. "It stops now."

This had already gotten out of hand. Damned if

his family was going to corner him into a relationship—no matter how much he wanted Hannah. She wasn't the kind of woman who would fit into his world, and there was no way he could fit into hers. And hell, that didn't make any sense even to him. Different worlds? Where were they, medieval England? No, it was more than that.

Just look at his parents. More than forty years together and they were at war. Hell, if they couldn't make it work, who the hell could? No, he didn't need that kind of upheaval. He had a life he'd built carefully on hard work and routine. Hannah didn't do routine.

She argued with him, was *amused* at his control and rigid adherence to schedules. She was as devoted to her company as he was to his, so how could they make that work? Always at odds over whose job came first? That sounded terrible.

She was funny and strong and confident, and she hit him on a level no other woman ever had. He wanted her, but that wasn't enough for him to stay involved. So. Better to end it now.

He should have been happy about that decision.

He wasn't.

The second week of the job was over and they were getting much closer to the finish line. *Really impressive*, Hannah thought, *what unlimited overtime and the promise of a bonus could do*. She sat back on her heels and looked around.

The floors had been sanded and covered with a tarp again to protect them until they could be refinished. The new cabinets were in, but the counters were still being made. The framing in the attic was almost complete and the work on the roof had been completed.

And she hadn't seen Ben since the night she'd experienced the best sex of her life. Since the night she'd been forced to admit to herself that she was in love with a man who would have no interest in hearing how she felt.

"Why hasn't he been checking up on me? Does he suddenly trust me?" She snorted at the very thought. "No. He's hiding from me."

Part of her actually enjoyed knowing he was scared, while most of her was just angry. Hard to imagine a grown man *hiding* from a woman because there was a danger to his oh-so-scheduled rut.

"Talking to yourself is never a good sign."

She smiled and looked to the doorway where her father stood, leaning against the doorjamb, watching her.

"I'm the only one who truly understands me," she quipped, knowing it wouldn't placate him.

"Oh, I don't know," he said, pushing off to walk to her. He sat down on the floor beside her and said, "I think I understand you pretty well."

Hannah sighed. There was no keeping things from Hank Yates. "You do. Always have."

He reached out and tapped her nose with his index finger. "Uh-huh. Which is how I know you're in love with Bennett Carey."

"Don't be silly." She looked away because she couldn't meet those eyes of his and not confess everything.

"You've never lied to me before. Be a shame to start now."

"Oh, Dad," she said, shaking her head. "How could I possibly love a man so rigid? So married to a schedule that he wears his gold watch to *bed*?" She winced a little as she'd pretty much just told her father she'd slept with Bennett Carey. Then she rushed on with more questions and complaints. "He owns a bazillion suits and *two* pairs of jeans. Can you imagine?"

"No, I actually can't."

"Me, either," she agreed with a sharp nod. "He checks up on me—or at least he *did*, every ten seconds, and now all of a sudden, bam, he's gone? What? I suddenly became trustworthy?"

"You don't think so."

"No, I don't. I think he's staying away on purpose and I don't care. Well," she amended, "I shouldn't care. And I don't."

"Okay, good," Hank soothed.

Her head fell back. "How can you fall in love in a *week*? That's ridiculous."

"Time's got nothing to do with it." He looked over

at her and smiled. "Took me two years to fall in love with your mother. And look how that turned out."

"Dad…" She laid her hand on his.

"That wasn't a bid for sympathy. I don't regret a thing, Hannah. How could I when I have you?" He smiled again, then added, "My point is, I had to work myself into love. I feel like, if it just drops on you, unexpectedly, that's how you know it's real."

She thought about that for a minute or two and wondered if he was right. But even if he was, what did that mean for her?

"All that said," her father continued, "I don't want to see you in the same kind of mess you were in with Davis."

"This is different, Dad." Wasn't it?

"I don't know. Davis used you. So is Bennett, in his own way."

Well, that caught her attention. "How?"

"By manipulating you into taking this job. By waving his money at you to get you to jump."

"No, that wasn't manipulation." Hannah shook her head. "I knew what I was doing. With that bonus, I can pay off Davis, invest in the company and give a little extra to the guys who work for us."

"I know all that. But I'm asking. Bennett was here every day, checking on the work. On *you*. Now he hasn't been here in a week. Why?"

"I told you, I think he's hiding from me."

"Doesn't say much for the man," he mused.

"I don't know. I guess I could understand why he's avoiding me if I wasn't so mad about it."

"Really?"

"It really doesn't matter anyway, Dad." She shook her head and let go of all the hurt and the anger and the resentment that she'd been holding against Ben. "There's nothing I can do about it. If he wants to ignore me, shouldn't I let him?" Of course she should. "Why should it be up to me to go hunt him down and make him talk to me?"

Hank shrugged, crossed his feet at the ankles and said, "Well, that's a question. I'm not saying I trust the guy, but if you love him, are you willing to let him walk away? If you love him, don't you deserve to have him face you and say whatever it is he's avoiding saying?" He turned his head to meet her eyes. "If you love him, are you willing to settle for less?"

Hannah tipped her head to his shoulder and found the comfort there that she'd always found with her father. "If you don't trust him, why are you saying all of this?"

"Because I trust you." He patted her hand and said softly, "Because I love you and I want you to be happy. If that means this guy…well, if he hurts you, we'll still have words. But I'm on your side, kiddo. Always."

"I know that, Dad," she whispered. "Thanks. I just don't know what I should do."

"Since when?" He laughed a little. "You've always

known what you want and I've never seen you back down. Are you really going to start now?"

He was right. But dealing with Ben was different. He was a man she never would have met if not for this job. They lived in two separate worlds, and when worlds collide, things could get ugly.

But did they have to collide? Couldn't they just sort of meet in the middle? Didn't she owe it to herself to find out?

Bennett was getting ready for a meeting when his cell phone rang. He glanced at the screen, then sat down at his desk again to answer. "Justin. Here's a surprise."

His younger brother was the ghost in the Carey family. There, but not present. He skipped more family meetings than he attended. He wasn't involved in the company business at all and made no secret of the fact that he wasn't in the slightest bit interested.

Bennett loved his brother, but with everything going on at the moment, he didn't have much patience for him.

"Yeah, Bennett, I need to talk to you."

"Great," he said, leaning back in his chair and studying the ceiling. "There's a family meeting in a half hour. Why don't you join us?"

"I'm in La Jolla."

A two-hour drive that on the 5 freeway could become a four-hour drive. "Right. Okay, well, I do have to be at the meeting."

"You have a half hour," Justin reminded him. "I only need a few minutes."

"Fine." Bennett waited while his brother went silent, and he didn't like not having his mind constantly occupied. The minute nothing was going on, his brain filled with images of Hannah. A week since he'd seen her. A week since the most amazing night of his life. But it wasn't just the sex that held him captivated, it was the woman herself. He'd never known anyone like her. Strong and funny and impatient. It was a damned intriguing combination. And he missed seeing her. Missed that smile of hers and the way her green eyes lit up when she looked at him. Missed everything about her, and that's why he wasn't going to think about her.

Scowling, he interrupted Justin's musings and demanded, "What is it?"

"Okay," he said, "I know we've got our problems, but I need your help."

Instantly, Bennett's demeanor changed. He sat up and asked, "Are you all right?"

"Yeah, I'm fine. I just…" He blew out a breath. "Hell, Bennett, I need a loan."

"Money? This call's about money?" That frown carved itself into his face. "Damn it, Justin…"

"I know. If I was a part of the company…"

"I wasn't going to say that."

"But you're thinking it," his brother muttered.

Yes, he was. "How much?"

Justin told him and Bennett choked. "Seriously?"

"I know it's a lot. But I need it to seal the deal I've been working on."

"What kind of deal?" Bennett asked the question they'd all been wondering about.

"I can't tell you. Yet," he added quickly. "But it's big, I can tell you that. Look, Bennett, I'll pay the loan back to the company at the end of next month. I've got trust money due then, and it's all yours."

Bennett would lend his brother the money, of course. There wasn't a question of that. They were all Careys. But this time there was going to be a price tag. "Look, I'll give you the money on one condition."

"Damn it, Bennett."

"Hear me out." Hell, Justin needed him, and Bennett didn't want to waste a golden opportunity. "You come to the Summer Stars dinner in two weeks, and the money's yours."

"What? Why?"

"Because you're a Carey, Justin," Bennett told him on a sigh. "Whether or not you want to be involved in the company, you *are* involved in the family. I want you there, so the Careys can present a united front. It's a big night for all of us."

There was a long pause as Justin considered it,

though Bennett knew damn well he'd go for it. He needed the money.

"It would mean a lot to Mom."

"That's fighting dirty."

Bennett grinned and wished his brother could see it. "I know. And, one more thing. I want you to convince Mom to move out of my house."

Justin laughed, and Bennett sneered at the phone.

"You realize this is blackmail," Justin finally said.

"What's your point?"

"Okay, fine. It's a deal," Justin said. "I'll be there. Where's the dinner being held?"

"The Carey."

Justin gave a long, low whistle. "The fire damage has been repaired already?"

"It will be." Again, Hannah raced through his mind. He waited a second until his thoughts cleared. "So, you'll be there?"

"I'll be there. I make no promises about Mom, though. She's not going to listen to any of us as long as Dad's not cooperating."

"You're the baby in the family. Use your power wisely."

Laughing, Justin said, "Agreed. You'll transfer the money today?"

"You'll have it this afternoon."

"Thanks, Bennett. I owe you."

"Damn straight you do. Pay me back at the dinner."

When he hung up and his assistant buzzed in,

Bennett muttered a curse. He checked his watch and shrugged. "What is it, David?"

"There's a Hannah Yates here to see you, sir."

His heart gave a hard jolt, and everything inside him twisted into what felt like a giant knot. A week since he'd seen her and it had taken everything in him to stay away from the restaurant. He'd made calls. Checked in. Even had his assistant go in his place once. But he hadn't wanted to see Hannah. Because he couldn't risk her getting even deeper inside him. Because he knew that seeing her again wouldn't be enough. He'd have to touch her. Hold her. And he wasn't entirely sure he'd be able to let her go again.

Though his plan hadn't worked very well because he still saw her every night when he closed his eyes. He heard her laugh. Saw those brilliant green eyes. Caught her scent in his lungs and woke up aching for her. What the hell was that? Lust? No. Couldn't be. If it was just lust, he wouldn't have bothered to distance himself. He'd have been back at her place the day after that one spectacular night.

No, it was more and he didn't want to acknowledge it even to himself. They were too different. Too far apart. She didn't believe in watches. He lived by one. She wore jeans. His world was dominated by suits and elegance. Her laugh was loud and happy and he never found much to laugh at. At least he hadn't, until he'd met her.

He was a different man when he was with Hannah, and Bennett wasn't sure he even *knew* that man. It was unsettling and so, the easiest way to put things back the way they should be, he told himself, was to stay away from the one woman who rocked his world.

Yet now she was here. Why? He wouldn't find out unless he talked to her, which was just what he'd been avoiding for a week. *So are you going to keep hiding like a coward?* he asked himself.

"Send her in."

He stood up, buttoned his suit jacket and faced the door. When it opened, she stepped inside and Bennett's breath caught in his lungs. A part of him wondered what David had thought of Hannah Yates in her dark blue jeans, work boots and Yates Construction T-shirt. Of course she'd shown up as herself. Hannah didn't play games. Didn't pretend to be something she wasn't. Damned if he didn't like that about her.

Hell, he liked everything about her.

"What is up with you?" She snapped out the question and her green eyes shone like there were flames in the depths.

Yeah. He liked her.

"What do you mean?"

"Oh please." She walked across the room in short, fast strides that brought her to a stop right in front of him.

He caught her scent on his next breath, and for a

moment, he wondered if he'd ever truly be free of it. Or if he wanted to be.

"You know damn well why I'm here." She folded her arms beneath her small, yet perfect breasts and hitched one hip higher than the other. "You're not checking up on me anymore."

He laughed shortly. "I thought you hated that."

"Turns out I hate *not* being checked on more." She read his expression correctly because she added, "Yes. Surprised me, too."

God, he'd missed her. He'd known it of course. The last week, he'd done little more than think about her, dream about her, and he'd told himself it was just the desire pumping inside him. But it was more. So much more that he reeled back from the knowledge of it.

There she stood, facing him down, glaring at him with those emerald eyes of hers and it was taking everything he had not to grab her up and take that mouth of hers in a kiss that would sear both of them. And what would be the point? When the job was finished, he wouldn't see her again. The Carey had brought them together, and when it was completed, it would end that connection, as well. Bennett needed to get back to the life he understood with his lists and schedules. Hannah was a disruption to all of that. And Bennett needed that structure. He wasn't sure he knew how to live without it.

But then, he didn't know if he could live without her, either. Or the fire they shared and that he couldn't stop thinking about.

"I've got more to keep track of than the restaurant."

"Uh-huh. That didn't stop you before."

"Hannah, what do you want to hear?"

She tipped her head to one side and fixed her green eyes on his. He couldn't have looked away even if he'd wanted to—and he really didn't want to.

"I want you to admit that you miss me. That it scares the crap out of you how much you miss me," she said, moving closer, keeping her gaze locked with his. "And I want you to admit that you haven't been able to stop thinking about me."

"If I did, what does that accomplish?" he wondered.

"It's honesty, Ben. The least we owe each other is that."

"You want honest?" He moved through the last few inches separating them and took hold of her shoulders. "Fine. I want you. I want you all the damn time and it's pissing me off."

She grinned and something in his chest simply melted. Was it his heart or just the ice that he'd kept that organ encased in?

"That's a good start," Hannah said.

"I stayed away because I had to. For my own sanity." He pulled her up onto her toes. His insides were jumping, his heart racing and he couldn't deny that seeing her again had suddenly made everything right again. And that made him mad, too. "What's between us is heat, but it's the kind that will burn itself out."

"How do you know?" she asked, her eyes spearing into his.

"That's what happens when a fire burns too hot."

"Not if you keep stoking it," she whispered. "Why don't we see how long it will burn?"

Tempting. Oh, so tempting. But then, everything about her tempted him. Bennett couldn't get enough of her even while telling himself he'd already had too much.

"And if we both get enveloped by the flames?"

Her mouth curved and the want that twisted inside him grew exponentially. This had never happened to him. This pulsing desire that only seemed to get bigger and bigger. Always before, Bennett could have a woman he desired and walk away clean, leaving her in the past, knowing that they'd both been satisfied with what they'd shared. He never lost control with a woman because none of them, he realized, had meant a damn thing to him.

Now though, Hannah Yates had crept into every corner of his mind, his body. He saw her and wanted her. Away from her, he wanted her. And he saw no end in sight. If the fire did burn itself out, wouldn't it be better to at least warm himself with it while it lasted? Could he walk away now, knowing that those flames were still hot enough to scorch them both?

"Being enveloped doesn't sound so bad," she whispered.

"This is a mistake, Hannah."

"And you never make mistakes, Ben?"

He rubbed his hands up and down her arms, feeling the strength in her, loving the hard, sculpted lines of her. Her short black hair against her white skin was alluring, and the gleam in her eyes drew him ever deeper.

"I guess I'm about to," he said softly, then bent his head to catch her mouth with his.

Instantly, she was all in. No coyness. No pretense of shyness. She gave all she was and let him know that they were in this together—wherever it led. Business, meetings, schedules, drained from his mind as he was filled with Hannah. A week, and it was as if it had been a year since he'd touched her.

Sunlight played in the room and the shush of the air conditioner sighed in the background, but all he could focus on was *her*. He couldn't have her here, in his office, as much as he might want to. But that didn't mean he couldn't at least touch her. He swept one hand down the length of her, and when she arched into him, he cupped the center of her and felt her response right down to his bones. Bennett felt her heat against his hand, right through the fabric of her jeans, and that heat ratcheted up what was already simmering inside him.

She held nothing back. Not even here, in his office, with the world right outside that closed door. Rocking her hips against his hand, she whimpered and a moan slid from her throat as he continued to ravage her mouth with his own. His blood was boiling and he couldn't imagine why he had thought staying away from her was a good idea. Nothing was better than this. Being with her. Touching her. Feeling her body coil in expectation.

He kissed her as she came, swallowing the choked whimpers sliding from her throat, and when finally, she went limp against him, he pulled his head back, smiled down into glassy, emerald green eyes and said, "I'll come to your house tonight."

"Yeah," she agreed on a sigh. "Good idea. You can finish what you started."

One corner of his mouth lifted. "Well, you know how I am about wanting jobs completed."

"I love a man with a schedule."

He smiled then and wondered why he hadn't recoiled from the word *love*.

"You should really do that more often," she said, reaching up to cup his face between her palms. "Smile, I mean. I'll see what I can do about that tonight."

"Might take a while," he warned.

"I finish the jobs I start," she said, and headed to the closed door.

Before she could open it and sail out of the office entirely, he spoke up. "Hannah. Come with me. To the awards dinner at the restaurant."

She turned to look at him and he could see the question in her eyes. He didn't know if he was giving her the answer she wanted, but he said, "I want you there. With me."

Hannah watched him for a long moment before finally nodding. "I want to be there. With you."

His assistant buzzed in. "Mr. Carey, they're waiting for you in the conference room."

He hit the answering button. "Tell them I'll be late."

Hannah's eyes went wide, and she gave him the grin that made him think of her as a sexy pixie. His heart rolled over, then thundered in his chest.

"I like you tossing aside the schedule," she admitted.

"You're making it too easy."

"No," she said, turning the doorknob slowly, "it's not just me, Ben. You're enjoying it."

When she was gone, he had to admit it... She was right.

Ten

For the next two weeks, they were together and Hannah told herself that it wouldn't end. Lying with him in her bed every night, making scrambled eggs and toast for dinner, or bringing home Chinese, they sat on her bed and picnicked naked and it was perfect. Her father had been right, she thought, when he'd told her to go after what she wanted, and still, she held back.

She never said the one word she knew might shatter what they had.

Love.

Ben hadn't said it, but she hadn't expected him to. He was the kind of man who looked at everything from every possible angle and tried to find the best way to handle a situation, no matter how long it might take. And she knew that *love* wasn't in his plans or on his schedule. He cared. She knew that. Felt that. But love from him remained elusive.

Yet, the restaurant was finished. The job complete. The bonus awarded and she was finally free of Davis. Her crew had the extra cash she'd promised them, and she'd already purchased some of the new equipment she'd dreamed about.

Now she had to wrestle with the situation she was in with Bennett Carey.

Hannah was impatient. She wanted more from him than just being her lover. She wanted the *L* word. Wanted tomorrow and the next day and the day after that. If that made her greedy or selfish, then she'd just have to live with it. The last two weeks had been everything she'd ever dreamed of having in her life, and she hated the thought that now the job was done what she shared with Ben might be ending.

When he rolled to one side and drew her up close, wrapping one arm around her, she snuggled in and listened to the hard thump of his heartbeat. This was what she wanted. Needed. But did she have the nerve to say so? Even as she thought it, she realized she had called Ben a coward for hiding from her and what he felt for her. But wasn't she doing the same thing now?

She wasn't brave enough to tell him she loved him. She wanted to be—she just wasn't there yet.

"I don't know if I've ever told you, but I like your house," he murmured, fingers running through her short hair.

Unexpected. She knew what kind of place he must be used to, though she'd never seen his home. She tipped her head back to look at him. "Thanks."

He smiled. He did that more often now and still she treasured every one. "Like your bedroom for instance…"

Hannah laughed. "Yeah, I know you like this room."

He gave her a hard hug. "I like the color. This deep—what is it called?"

"Burgundy."

"Right. Well, it's nice. Restful, sort of gives the room a quiet cave-like feel."

"Oh, that's nice!"

"You know what I mean. It's intimate. Cozy, somehow. You should hear my sisters and mother go on about my house. *Beige, Bennett. No one likes beige.*"

"They're right." She lifted her head, braced her arm on his chest and took the opportunity to ask, "Why do we never go to your house?"

Moonlight drifted through the gap in the curtains and lay across his face, so she watched his features tighten. "Because, my mother's living there. She's punishing my father for not retiring as he promised, and she refuses to leave."

"And you don't want to introduce me," she said, and hoped he didn't hear the hurt in her voice.

"That's not exactly it," he argued. "She drives me crazy, Hannah."

"You're lucky," she said.

"And you don't know my mother," he said, trying for lighthearted and failing.

A quick jab of pain because he never took her around his family. It was as if this side of him, this thing they shared, was to be kept secret. Guarded from everyone. Why?

"I'd like to," she said.

"Hannah…"

"I know." She sat up and looked down at him. "No one knows we're together like this. We don't see my friends or your family. We hide what we are to each other and sneak around like teenagers."

"I don't consider it hiding," he argued. "I consider it private."

"From your family?"

He laughed shortly. "Especially from my family."

"Great." That hurt pooling inside her widened and deepened. *Especially his family.* Pushing off the bed, she switched on a bedside light, and the soft, golden glow of the bulb had Ben tossing one arm across his eyes like a vampire reeling back from a cross.

A moment later, he lowered his arm, then held out one hand to her, silently asking her to join him again.

She sat on the edge of the bed and took his hand, but forced herself to ask, "Are you ashamed of me?"

"What?" Pure astonishment colored his tone and etched itself across his features. "Where the hell did that come from?"

"The hiding."

He blew out a breath, and frustration was in his voice when he said, "It's not you, Hannah. It's my mom. If I took you to the house, she'd assume we were…"

"What? Together?" she asked, as the first stirrings of anger began to bubble inside her. "Aren't we?"

He scowled, an expression she was all too familiar with. "Of course we are, but she would think that it was more than it is."

"I see." Her voice sounded cold, even to her. Amazing how quickly pain could turn to outrage. "Why don't you explain to me what *this* is, exactly, Ben?"

He pushed both hands through his hair in a show of exasperation. And when he spoke, he didn't answer her. "How did we get onto this anyway?"

"I met your sisters," she reminded him, ignoring his question in favor of her own.

"Yeah, I know. They're still talking about you, asking questions."

"And what do you tell them?" This was important. To her. To them. Couldn't he see that?

"Nothing," he admitted. "I don't talk about my private life with them, Hannah."

Disappointment warred with the anger and not surprisingly, anger won the day.

"That's what family is for, Ben. Talking to them about the important things in your life."

"That's not who I am, Hannah. You know that."

"What I know is," she said with a shake of her head, "instead of being impatient with your mother, you should be appreciating having her in your life."

He snorted.

"I mean it. My mother left my dad and me when I was barely old enough to walk." His smile faded and his eyes fixed on hers. "She decided she didn't want to be a wife. A mother. And left to find her own joy. Never saw her again. Do you know what it would mean to me to have a mother who wanted to know what was happening in my life?"

"Hannah…"

"No, it's fine. I'm fine." She got off the bed again because she thought better on her feet. Looking down at him, she drew his features into her brain so that no matter what happened next, she would always be able to see him when she closed her eyes. "The thing is, Ben, you should know that this…thing, between us? It's more than just temporary for me."

She could see the wariness in his gaze even before he said, "Hannah, don't."

Hannah had come too far now, and she wouldn't

stop even if she could have. She was through being a coward. She'd gone to his office, hadn't she? Well, she needed that kind of courage now, too. "Too late. I should have said something before. But somehow I was afraid that if I did, it would all end. Now I realize though, if I don't say something, it *will* end, because something in me will die." She took a breath, met his gaze squarely and said, "I love you, Ben. I have almost from the start."

"Damn it, Hannah." Now he pushed off the bed and stood staring at her across the mattress. "You don't mean that."

"Don't tell me what I mean. I said *love* and I meant *love*." At the look on his face, she muttered, "Though at the moment, I couldn't tell you *why* I love you."

"Exactly. You can't. We have nothing in common, Hannah."

"That's too easy, Ben." She snatched up her short, pale blue robe from a nearby chair and shrugged it on. "If you don't want to feel something for me, have the guts to admit it. Things in common? What does that even mean? No.

"I've done a lot of thinking about this, too. I know you're the rich guy, living in a beige house that you're never in. I'm the contractor living in a brightly colored tiny house that you already admitted you like."

"That's—"

"We both love our families. We're both hard workers. We both have big plans. And what we have here?" She waved a hand at the bed with the rumpled sheet and duvet. "That's magic, Ben. And you damn well know it. So if you don't want me, just say so, but don't give me those pale reasons for backing away."

"I do want you," he admitted. "Always will. But I don't even know if I'm capable of what you're wanting from me."

"You'll never know if you don't try."

"Maybe I don't want to know."

Nodding, blinking fast to keep the tears gathering in her eyes from falling, Hannah said, "Well. That's honest, anyway. I really think you should go now, Ben."

She'd taken her shot. Told him how she felt, even knowing that it would probably end just as it had. But she wouldn't regret it. Wouldn't second-guess herself for falling in love with Bennett Carey. Love wasn't a decision to make. It just… *Was*.

"I don't want to leave you like this, Hannah."

"But you do want to leave, so you really should." She walked out of her bedroom, headed for the kitchen. He could get dressed and leave on his own. God knew, he'd spent enough time here to be able to find the damn door without her.

"All set for the Summer Stars celebration?" Amanda dropped into one of the visitor chairs in Bennett's office and crossed her legs.

"Of course I'm set," he answered, barely looking at his sister. "Why wouldn't I be set?"

The damn celebration. At the damn restaurant that Hannah had restored not only to its former glory but to something it should always have been. Sure. He'd love to be there. Without her.

"Well, of course," Amanda mused. "I can hear the joy in your voice."

He lifted his gaze and scowled at her.

"Oh please, like the death stare is going to work." Amanda waved one hand at him dismissively. "I'm your sister, Bennett. I've seen your 'go away' stare since you were ten."

"And yet, you remain." Deliberately he lowered his gaze to the papers in front of him and tried to see them as more than black smudges on a white background.

"How's Hannah?"

"Why ask me?"

"Because I have cleverly deduced that you've made a mess of things with her and that's why you've become a human Death Star wandering these illustrious corridors."

"Do you *practice* being annoying?" He tossed his pen down and leaned back in his chair.

"No practice required," she quipped. "It's a gift."

"Return it."

"Oh, a joke. Very exciting." Amanda leaned forward, speared her gaze into his and asked, "What did you do?"

"I didn't do a damn thing."

"That's what they all say."

"Damn it, Amanda, butt out."

"Not going to happen."

"She said she loves me," he blurted, then wished with everything inside him he could call it back.

"Oh, Bennett," she said on a sigh. "That's not news to anyone but you."

"You might've told me." He stood up, walked to the wall of windows and stared out at the sea.

"It wouldn't have helped."

No, it wouldn't have. He could admit that, at least to himself. God, he could still see her, standing beside her bed, wearing nothing but moonlight. Everything in him yearned for her. Probably always would. But he saw his parents now, at war after nearly forty years. Living with someone wasn't easy in the best of times, and he wasn't an easy man at *any* time. How long before he and Hannah made each other miserable? How long before their differences tore them apart?

Wasn't it easier to end it now rather than years from now when there might be kids involved? Hell, his parents had been together forever. It hadn't always been sunshine and roses, either. He remembered arguments. Hard words and cold silences—and the two of them had shared common ground. If it was hard for *them*, how much harder would it be for him and Hannah?

Bennett turned to look at his sister. "I appreciate the concern, but it's done, Mandy. Finished. And we'll just have to deal with it."

"I love you, Bennett, but sometimes, you're so male, I just want to clock you." She stood up, smoothed her skirt and shook her head. "You're making a mistake, you know."

"Funny. I said the same thing to Hannah not so long ago."

"She should have listened," Amanda murmured.

"Yeah," Bennett said when his sister was gone. "She should have."

Hannah took her measurements, then noted them on her tablet. When she had the second set of measurements, she did the same, and then measured everything again just to make sure.

The sun was streaming down on Jack Colton's backyard and the roar of the sea was like a throaty purr in the background. The wind kicked at her, just to make maneuvering her measuring tape more interesting. Looking at the length of the backyard made her smile.

Not only was Yates Construction going to build a real stone castle—kid-sized, of course—but Jack wanted a retaining wall along the property to make sure his new daughter wouldn't go racing off a cliff.

"Good policy," she said to herself.

"I always trust people who talk to themselves."

Hannah whirled around and watched an older woman in a beautiful, pale green jacket and skirt walk across the lawn toward her. She had short, chestnut-colored hair, blue eyes and a soft smile curving her mouth. And Hannah had a very good idea who the woman was.

"You're Ben's mother."

"I am," she said with a broader smile. "How did you know?"

"He has your eyes."

"Isn't that nice of you to say? Please. Call me Candace. And you're Hannah." She tipped her head to one side as if to study her more closely. "I have to confess that I came here specifically to meet you."

Instantly, Hannah wished she were dressed better for the occasion. Her Yates Construction T-shirt, blue jeans and work boots probably weren't making the best of impressions. Yet even as she thought it, she realized it didn't matter. This was who she was. If that wasn't good enough for the Careys, then too damn bad. Besides, Ben wasn't in her life anymore, and that thought brought a sinking sensation to the pit of her stomach.

It had only been two days since he'd walked out of her house—her life—and it felt like years. She couldn't imagine what surviving the coming years would be like. Empty, emptier, emptiest.

"It's nice to meet you," she finally said when she realized she'd been quiet too long.

"Oh, you don't think so at the moment," the other woman said, reaching out to pat her hand. "But you will. For me, I'm enjoying it."

"Happy to help."

She laughed. "Oh yes. Definitely enjoying it. Please, let's sit down for a second. Jack told me you'd be here, checking the property for Alli's castle."

That's right. "Alli's your granddaughter."

"Yes, and don't encourage me, I have hundreds of photos on my phone and I'll bore you brainless."

Hannah relaxed. It was impossible to remain stiff and uncomfortable around this woman. Ben was stupid to complain about her.

She followed Candace to a low stone bench tucked beneath a shade tree. When she sat down, Candace said, "Oh, Alli is going to love that castle. Do you have a design for it yet?"

"Yeah, actually. The architect is working on the plans now. When he's finished, we'll start. Should have the permits by next week, and then we'll be good to go."

Candace shook her head and the dappled sunlight caught the highlights in her hair. "I'm so impressed by you."

"You are?" That she hadn't expected.

"Oh yes. A woman running a construction company? That's very admirable."

"Well, thank you."

"My daughter Mandy tells me you love my son."

"Quite the segue."

Candace waved a manicured hand absently. "No point in not talking about it, is there?"

"I suppose not." Hannah shifted on the bench to look at the other woman squarely. "It doesn't matter now anyway. I did love him. But I'll get over it."

In twenty or thirty years. She turned her face into the sea breeze and let it ruffle her short, dark hair. Anything to keep from seeing sympathy on Candace's face. She didn't need it or want it.

She didn't get it, either.

"I don't think you should try."

"No offense, Candace," Hannah said quietly, "but you don't get a vote."

She laughed at that and nodded. "True, I don't. But you can't stop me from wishing." She reached out and laid one hand on Hannah's arm. "Bennett is just miserable."

"Yes," she said wryly. "I know."

Another chuckle. "You're perfect for him, I swear."

As much as she liked the sound of that, Hannah said, "No, I'm not. Ask him. He'll tell you."

"Hannah, you are the first woman to ever befuddle my son."

"Befuddle?" Hannah shook her head. "If you asked him, Ben would say I infuriated, frustrated and annoyed him. But I don't think he'd say befuddled."

"That's exactly why you're perfect for him."

"You're not making sense." And she wondered how she could get out of this conversation. Hannah gave a quick look around, but the expansive yard was empty. Not even a damn gardener there to distract Candace. Funny. Suddenly, Hannah understood why Bennett was being driven to distraction by his mother. A hammer, even a velvet-wrapped hammer, could do some damage.

"You don't understand, Hannah." The woman took a breath, looked around the backyard herself, then shifted her gaze until she met Hannah's. "Bennett's always been so stern. So controlled. It was as if he were born wearing an Armani suit—which I can testify he was not."

Hannah smiled.

"It's his nature to be controlling," she continued. "To look after everyone and everything, so that he's never felt he had the right to take something for himself.

"Maybe some of that is our fault," Candace mused. "He is the oldest and so responsible right from the start that we were constantly putting him in charge of his siblings while we were working on the business."

"I don't think that's so unusual," Hannah said.

"Maybe not, but," she added with another smile, "when you're a mother, you'll realize that your full-time hobby becomes looking back and wondering if you did things right. If you should have done them differently and how that might have affected your children." She took a breath and said, "But that's not why I'm here."

"Why are you here?" Hannah asked.

"Because you love my son," Candace said. "And I want that for him. He deserves to be loved and to love in return."

"Yes, well," Hannah said, wishing she were anywhere but there. "I think so, too. But he, unfortunately, doesn't. So while I appreciate the thought, Candace—"

"You wish I would go away."

Hannah opened her mouth, but what could she say? So she closed it again.

Candace chuckled and pushed her windblown hair back from her face. "You're a nice woman, Hannah. Too nice to tell me to mind my own business. But I'm going to say what I came here to say. Don't give up on him. He's worth the trouble."

She would love to think that Ben's mother was right. That all he needed was time to see that they were meant to be together. But how could she believe that when she'd seen for herself how the mere mention of the word *love* had shut him down completely? And there was the "nothing in common" argument, as well.

"You're coming to the Summer Stars celebration tomorrow night, aren't you?"

Hannah frowned and shook her head. "I was going to but now I think—"

"Good. I'll expect you to be there." Candace stood up and brushed off the seat of her skirt. "It's as much your celebration as anyone's, isn't it? The chance to showcase the work you and your company did. I've toured the restaurant and I'm very impressed with your skills and talents."

"Thank you," Hannah said as she stood up. "That's nice to hear but—"

"Hannah," the older woman said gently. "Do you want him to think you were too afraid to face him?"

"Oh, you're very clever," Hannah said after a second or two. "I bet it was impossible for your kids to get anything past you."

Candace smiled. "Not impossible. But certainly not easy. So. I'll see you tomorrow night?"

She shouldn't, of course. She should stay far, far away from Ben Carey. But as she looked at his mother, Hannah knew she wasn't going to do that. She would go to that party, and she would look so good, he'd eat his heart out.

"I like the gleam in your eye, Hannah," Candace said with a wink. "I think the two of us are going to get along very well together."

The Carey was better than ever.

Bennett stood alone near the bar and watched the crowd move through the restaurant and every last one of them couldn't stop talking about the changes. The improvements.

Even the floors were stunning—the lighter stain lifted the entire atmosphere of the place. Hannah had been right about that. Fresh paint in a soft rose color lightened the walls and made the new, lighter tables look like circles of privacy. Flowers graced every table and the larger, banquette tables along one wall. Hannah had been right about that, too, as she'd been about the cream-colored leather.

The kitchen was a damn masterpiece, he had to admit because John Henry hadn't stopped raving about it since the completion. Hannah had talked to the chef, made suggestions and ended up by moving the workstations around to create an easier flow for the chefs and waiters to navigate.

She'd done everything she said she would. She'd delivered first-class work under a killer deadline. She was right about every suggestion she'd made. He missed her. Hell, just seeing his restaurant made him think of her, and that was a nightmare because he was here all the damn time. So she'd be haunting him for the rest of his life.

Bennett's skin seemed to buzz, as if the air itself was suddenly electrified. His gaze swept the room and he spotted her. Here. In the restaurant. Just inside the door. Yes, he'd invited her, but after that last night at her house, he hadn't expected to see her tonight. Now that she was here, though, he suddenly felt as if he could breathe again. As if the invisible iron bands around his chest had loosened, he drew one long breath and would have sworn he could smell her, even from a distance. Sense memory brought her scent to him, and Bennet hung on to it even as he indulged in a long, leisurely perusal.

She wore an emerald green, strapless dress that clung to her upper body, then fell into a swirl around her legs, stopping just above her knees. Silver links dangled from her earlobes and as she watched the crowd, she wore a small smile that tugged at everything inside him. She was breathtaking.

Bennett threaded his way through the crowd and around the press taking pictures of the Summer Stars winners. When she spotted him, he noticed her chin come up, and he hated that she instinctively made that defensive move.

"You look amazing," he said, his voice pitched low, in spite of the noise in the room.

"Thanks." She tipped her head back to look up at him, and he noticed that her eyes looked a deeper green tonight. Like a forest in the starlit dark. "So do you."

He wanted to touch her. Hell, he wanted to taste her, sink into the feel of her pressed against him. Instead, he took another long breath and prayed for control. "Everyone's talking about how great the restaurant looks."

"Not everyone," she said, and nodded toward the

press gathered around a young man and woman, smiling for photographs.

"Ah. Jacob Foley and his sister Sheila," he said. "They won the competition by a few thousand votes. They do sort of Celtic music. Guitar, violin and Sheila sings. They're pretty amazing actually."

"And now they get to perform at the Carey Center one night this summer?"

"That's right." He looked down at her. "We'll promote the hell out of it, and with any luck they can use that performance as a stepping-stone to a career."

"They're that good?"

"They really are. And, the contest was so popular we're going to do it every year, and I don't want to talk about the Summer Stars anymore." He stared down into her eyes and felt his world right itself. That thought both comforted and horrified him. When did she become so damned important? So essential?

"I'm glad you're here."

"Why?"

He choked out a laugh. "Trust you to ask that. Answer's simple. Because I missed you."

"Good. I missed you, too."

Bennett smiled.

"I got a smile out of you, too."

"Not many can," he admitted. He crooked his arm, then threaded her hand through it. "Let me introduce you around."

For the next half hour, Bennett kept her close to

his side and introduced her to dozens of people. They made small talk, as always happened at those sorts of things. And through it all he sensed Hannah pulling further and further away from him in spite of the fact that he had her arm in his. He couldn't figure out what was wrong.

Finally though, he found her a chair at a table and left to get glasses of champagne for both of them, hoping that once they had a chance to talk they could find a way to get back to where they were just days ago. Before the love admission. Before everything had changed.

First, of course, he had to find out what was bothering her and try to fix it.

Hannah watched him go and buried the knot of disappointment lodged in her chest. She'd hoped… Stupid. Hopes were futile when confronted with stark reality. And the reality was, Ben was not the man for her. She watched him, and everything inside her ached for things to be different, but he'd just proven to her that nothing would change.

"So—" a voice brushed her ear "—Bennett Carey, huh?"

A cold, sinking sensation opened up in her chest. Hannah turned her head to meet Davis Buckley's cool stare. *The perfect capper to the evening*, she thought. Of course he would be here. The rich and the famous and the press were all over the restaurant. Davis would never miss an event like this one.

As she looked at him, she remembered that at one time, she'd thought Davis was the one, and yet, looking back now, what she had felt for him was such a pale imitation of what she felt for Bennett. It amazed her now to think that she ever could have thought she was in love with the man. He was so obviously... What was the word Amanda Carey had used? Oh right. Toady.

"What do you want, Davis?" Hannah asked, standing up to face him. The rumble of conversation around them was a counterpoint to their lowered voices. "I paid off your 'loan.' We're even. I don't owe you a thing. Not even a moment of my time."

Davis looked her up and down so dismissively, it was all she could do not to kick him. "Now I see why you dumped me. You were after a richer catch. Nice job, hooking Bennett Carey. Many have tried, no one's succeeded."

Astonished, she asked, "What are you talking about?"

"I saw him slavering over you." Davis snorted his disgust. "Do you think I'm stupid?"

"Among other things," Amanda said. "Go away, Davis. And stay away."

"Happy to," he said, looking past her. "Hello, Bennett. Good to see you."

Hannah felt her stomach simply drop. How long

had he been standing there? Had he heard them talking? Had he overheard Davis accusing her of dumping him for a "richer catch"? Slowly, she turned around to face the man who was looking at her as if he'd never seen her before. The answer to her question was written all over his face.

He'd heard every word.

"Bennett, it's not what you think."

Eleven

"Can't wait to hear what it actually is, then," Bennett said. Setting the champagne glasses down on the table, he grabbed her hand and headed for the front door. She didn't try to stop him. She wanted to have this out as much as he did. Maybe more.

Once outside, the sea wind slapped at them, but it didn't seem to cool the tempers spiking in each of them.

"Davis Buckley?" Bennett demanded. "You were involved with that slimeball?"

"Engaged, actually," she corrected, though the words tasted bitter on her tongue. He reeled back from that information and stuffed both hands into his pockets.

The parking lot was crowded—mostly expensive sports cars and SUVs, of course. The valets were running in and out, so Bennett steered her toward the side of the building where they could be private. Out of the corner of her eye, Hannah saw someone start toward them—probably hoping to speak to Bennett, then obviously reading the situation, the man suddenly veered away. She couldn't blame him.

Staring up into his eyes, she noticed that right now, they were the color of a stormy sky. Well, she felt the same way. Still, she told him everything. Explained about Davis and how naive she'd been and why she'd needed the job on The Carey and how the bonus had finally paid off her last loan with Davis. When she was finished, she waited for his reaction and it didn't take long.

"Oh, that's great!" He threw both hands up. "So you were 'in love' with him, too?"

She flinched at the sneer in his tone. "I thought I was, yeah. But it's nothing—"

"Let me guess. Nothing like you feel for me?" He shook his head, turned and walked away only to come right back. "Was he right? Did you use me like you used him?"

"Excuse me?" Hannah had had all she could take. She had been willing to cut him a little slack because Davis Buckley had to have been an ugly surprise. But she wouldn't stand there and let him put this all on her. "Davis was the one who used *me*. Like you have."

He snorted. "You can't be serious."

"Funny. Your sisters saw the truth. Why is it you can't?" She cocked her head, set both hands at her hips and said, "You used my skills and my crew's time to get your restaurant up and running for this self-congratulatory party where the combined wealth of your guest list would equal more than the GDP of some *countries*."

"I hired you. Didn't use you. And now it's a crime to be rich?"

"Of course not," she snapped, "but it should be a crime to be thoughtless about it."

"Thanks very much."

Did he not see it? she wondered, or did he not *want* to see it?

"Ben, you just spent a half hour dragging me around the restaurant, introducing me to all of your rich friends, but never once," she said tightly, "did you tell them that I'm the contractor who did the work on the restaurant. You didn't want them to know that I'm in charge of a crew of men. That I own a construction business."

Bennett scrubbed one hand across his face and shook his head. "That's not what this is about."

"It's exactly that." She stepped in closer, tapped his chest with her index finger and said, "When I told you I was in love with you, you gave me an argument about having nothing in common. But that's not what's driving you, Ben. It's the fact that you're *embarrassed* by what I do for a living."

"I never said that," he argued.

"You didn't have to," she told him and swallowed the hurt burning inside her. "Tonight, you just made it perfectly clear. I'm sorry I'm not some elegant rich woman who won't turn a doorknob for fear of ruining her manicure."

"You're being ridiculous."

"Am I? I don't think so." She did a slow turn, letting him get a good look at her. "This isn't the real me. Or at least it's not the *only* part of me. I wear work boots. I put up Sheetrock and whatever else needs doing on a job site. I take as much pride in my work as you do in yours. I'm running a family business. Just like you. And I'm damn good at what I do. What I *won't* do is waste my time on a man who's ashamed of who I am.

"Goodbye, Ben. Enjoy your party."

"Wait."

Hannah stopped and looked over her shoulder at him.

"Why did you come here tonight, Hannah?"

"Because I wanted to prove to myself I could face you again. And I wanted you to see me and eat your heart out."

"Well then. Mission accomplished."

That should have made her feel good. But it didn't. She left him standing there, and one of the valets called her a cab. While she waited, she looked back over her shoulder and saw that he was still standing in the dark, watching her. Her heart ached, but her spine stiffened.

When the cab arrived, she got in and went home. Alone.

That night, Bennett didn't sleep.

Every time he closed his eyes, he saw Hannah. Saw the flash of anger and hurt in her eyes. Heard her voice, calling him out. Remembered her telling him about being engaged to Davis Buckley, of all people. Was it *his* fault he'd been so shocked by that news that he'd reacted badly?

Yes.

By 7:00 a.m., he was on edge, exhausted and had a headache pounding behind his eyes. So when he heard live music right outside his house, he accepted it as just another form of torture. Pushing out of bed, he walked to the window, looked down and saw a band, complete with drum kit and amplifiers, playing, of all things "Love Will Keep Us Together."

Bennett's chin hit his chest.

Martin Carey was standing right behind the band, staring up at the house, grinning like a loon, obviously waiting for his wife to appear and be swept off her feet by his romantic gesture. Bennett knew that was his parents' song. It was popular when they were dating and when he was a kid, he'd sometimes caught his parents dancing to the song when they thought they were alone.

At the moment, several of his neighbors had come out of their homes and were now dancing to the music, enjoying the morning's surprise entertainment. It was over-the-top, completely unexpected and Bennett thought, he had to give it to his father. Maybe this would be the thing to finally get Candace to forgive him and move the hell out of Bennett's house.

So a few minutes later, when his mother stepped outside, dressed for work in a black-and-white shirt-dress and heels, Bennett damn near held his breath. Would she go for it?

No.

The band stopped playing and with his window open, Bennett actually heard the click of his mother's heels on the stone walk. She moved past the band as if they weren't there and stopped in front of Martin. "You just don't understand anything, do you, Marty? You really think playing our song will convince me to come home when nothing has really changed?"

"Candy, this has gone on long enough," his father complained.

"It certainly has," Candace agreed, then glanced at the band. "I'm ignoring your attempt. Not fun to be ignored, is it?"

With that, she slid into her BMW and drove off, leaving Martin and the band behind. The neighbors called out for more music, so the band started playing again and the party continued. Martin got in his car and left. Bennett closed the window, shutting the music down to a muffled roar.

His parents weren't solving this mess. And Bennett wondered what it was women actually *did* want. His mother wasn't impressed with a big romantic gesture. Hannah kept her relationship with Davis Buckley a secret—or had she? They hadn't talked about their pasts. Maybe she would have told him, but he probably would have reacted just as he had. And his sisters were on her side. Worse, Hannah had accused him of being ashamed of her.

He scowled and caught his own reflection in the mirror across from the bed. *Hard to lie to yourself when the truth is right there staring at you.*

"Damn it," he told the face staring back at him. "She was right. You were being a damn snob. You avoided telling people that *she* restored the restaurant, when in reality, you should have been proud to introduce a stunning woman who is so blasted talented she could build a house from the ground up by herself."

Had he become such an elitist that he couldn't see anyone's worth beyond their financial bottom line? Was a career or a business only worth admiring if it could be done in an expensive suit or elegant dress? That was a damned depressing thought. And humiliating.

As for Davis Buckley. Hell. Hannah had had the good sense to end that engagement—not to mention working her gorgeous ass off to pay back the man's loans so she could be free of him entirely. But had Bennett taken the time to realize that when it counted?

No.

He pushed one hand through his hair and yanked on that hair for good measure. What the hell was wrong with him? He had a beautiful woman tell him she loved him, and he accused her of trying to use him?

Instead of grabbing at his chance for love and happiness, he'd tossed it back in her face and embarrassed her by refusing to appreciate her for the amazing woman she was. Hell, his parents had been married forty years. Even now, with the Retirement Wars going on, there was no talk of divorce. They loved each other so much each was trying to convince the other to see things their way. How could he *not* believe in love with the Careys as an example?

Staring at his reflection, he jabbed one finger at the man in the mirror. "*You* are an idiot."

"You're an idiot, that's what you are," Hannah muttered darkly. She'd allowed herself to love Ben, and as it turned out, he might be even worse than Davis. At least Davis Buckley was up front about the kind of man he was. Ben had fooled her into thinking he was different. Sure, a little closed off and a walking frown, but a good guy.

But at the core of things, he was like every other rich client she'd ever known.

"And that's why you're an idiot," she said.

"What's that, boss?" Tiny pushed his hat back and squinted at her in the bright sunlight.

"Nothing," she assured him. "Just talking to myself."

"Hah, when I do that, my wife says I'm losing it." When she turned a steely stare on him, he quickly added, "I don't think that, of course."

"Right." She stared up at the back of the house they were working on. They had to cut away the eaves and part of the roof to attach the new front porch roof. This remodel was a good idea, she thought. They'd pour concrete in a day or two, giving the homeowners the kind of porch that had room for a few chairs and a table. The roof would afford protection from sunlight and rain and give their house the kind of character the original builder had decided against.

"Okay, you guys work on breaking up the old porch while I get to work on the eaves." She set the ladder to lean against the roof and started climbing while her crew took care of the demo on the ground.

"Uh, boss…"

"Tiny, just break up the concrete, okay?" She didn't want to talk. Not even to herself anymore. Talk didn't solve anything. Going over and over what had happened between her and Ben didn't solve anything, either.

"Boss, there's someone here to see you…"

She sighed, half turned on the ladder to watch Ben

cross the front yard to stand beneath her, looking up. Wearing one of his ever-present suits and very expensive shoes, he looked as out of place as she had felt at the big party at The Carey.

Oh, and it was humiliating to admit that even after everything they'd said to each other, Hannah's heartbeat still jittered when she saw him. Her pulse raced and everything in her wished things were different. But since they weren't, she would just wish he would leave.

"Go away, Ben. I'm working."

Bennett took a breath and scrubbed one hand across his jaw. He'd started his morning off by talking to Hannah's father, and that man had been as *welcoming* as her crew was at the moment. He understood their attitude. Hell, he'd caused it by bringing Hannah pain. What he *couldn't* take was the hurt in her eyes when she looked at him.

"I was wrong," he said, loud enough for everyone to hear over the sound of power tools. And as soon as he spoke, those tools were shut off, apparently so the crew wouldn't miss whatever happened next.

"I agree," she said, and kept climbing. "Now go away."

"Come down so we can talk," he said.

"I have nothing to say," she told him, and used the claw end of her hammer to peel up one of the eave boards. When she had it free, she tossed it to the ground, and he jumped back to avoid being hit.

"Almost got me," he said.

"I'll try harder next time," she told him.

He grinned briefly. Damn, he loved this woman.

"Okay that's it," Bennet muttered and started for the ladder. "If you won't come down, I'll come up."

"Do you have a death wish?" She looked down at him, stunned surprise on her face. "Get down before you upset the balance and kill us both."

"The balance is already upset Hannah," he said, keeping his gaze on her as he climbed. One of his feet slid off a rung and he made a mental note not to wear dress shoes the next time he climbed a ladder.

"Whose fault is that?" she asked.

"Mine," he admitted. It wasn't as difficult as he'd thought it would be, talking to her, telling her what he needed her to hear. All he had to do was go with his gut. "I was wrong. And careless. And short-sighted."

Someone on the crew applauded. Bennett ignored him.

"Damn it, Hannah," he said. "I love you. I'm proud of you and everything you can do. I love who you are. Your talent. Your pride. Your confidence. Your laugh. All I want is another chance to prove it."

She looked down at him, and he saw something in her eyes that gave him hope.

"I handled this all wrong, Hannah," he admitted,

ignoring the cheers and applause from her crew. He
knew her father was down there, too, listening, but
he wasn't speaking to any of them. Only one person mattered here. "I hurt you and I didn't mean to.
I didn't value you, and that will never happen again.
I love you, Hannah, and that will never change."

She turned, leaned one hip against a rung of the
ladder, and said, "Ben, I think I believe you, but that
doesn't change the reality. I don't belong in your
world any more than you belong in mine."

He smiled. "That's bull, Hannah, and you know
it. We make the worlds the way they are. And, I'd
like to point out that I'm in your world right now and
the universe didn't explode."

"Yet," she muttered.

Bennett grinned. "Hannah, we can build our own
place, the best of both our worlds and screw anyone
who tries to tell us differently. Be with me, Hannah. Love me. Make a family with me. I miss you.
I miss *us*."

Her gaze locked with his, and he felt her wants
and desires as surely as his own. How could he have
been so blind as to let her nearly slip away from him?

"I won't stop working, Ben. I want to grow my
company until we're the number one contracting
company in Southern California."

More cheers from the crew, and who could blame
them?

"That sounds great to me. You deserve nothing

less." More applause from the crew. "You can start by renovating my house because my whole family says it's boring."

"They're probably right," she said, lips twitching.

"It'll be a challenge," he said, smiling.

"*You're* the real challenge," she retorted.

"Agreed." He stared into her eyes, and said, "I'm as stubborn and single-minded as you are, so that might make for a bumpy road sometimes. But damn it, Hannah, I want to be on that road with you. Only with you. We can build a great life together."

"I want kids," she warned him.

"As many as we want."

"I'll teach them how to use tools," she said.

"Great. You can teach me at the same time."

Grinning now, Hannah looked over at her father. Ben followed her gaze and saw the older man give two thumbs-up. Then she turned her gaze back to Bennett, and when she leaned down to kiss him, he stopped her.

"Can we get down on the ground for the kissing part?"

She laughed, and the sound was like a musical balm to his soul. Once they were on their own two feet again, Bennett swept her into a hard embrace and kissed her until they were both breathless. And while the crew around them laughed and shouted, Bennett dug into his pocket for the ring he'd purchased only that morning.

"Channel set diamonds," she whispered, looking up at him.

He shrugged and slipped it onto her finger. "So nothing will get caught in machinery."

Hannah sighed, lifted one hand to cup his cheek and whispered, "I can't believe you thought of that."

Bennett held her tightly to him and murmured, "I will always think of you first. I will always love you. Forever and then beyond that."

Hannah smiled up at him and said, "I love you, Ben. Now and always. And to prove it, I promise to attend all of the fancy parties you want me to."

"And I promise not to use power tools unsupervised," he said.

"Thank God," she said, throwing herself at him, wrapping her arms around his neck and holding on.

When he held her tight and swung her in a circle, Bennett whispered, "Thank you. For loving me enough to change my world forever."

She looked down into his eyes and promised, "Forever, King Carey."

* * * * *

Look for Justin's story,
One Little Secret
Available next month!

COMING NEXT MONTH FROM

#2845 MARRIED BY CONTRACT
Texas Cattleman's Club: Fathers and Sons
by Yvonne Lindsay
Burned before, rancher Gabriel Carrington wants a marriage on paper. But when one hot night with fashionista Rosalind Banks ends in pregnancy, he proposes...a deal. Their marriage of convenience could give them both what they want—if they can get past their sizzling chemistry...

#2846 ONE LITTLE SECRET
Dynasties: The Carey Center • by Maureen Child
Branching out from his wealthy family, black sheep Justin Carey pursued a business deal with hotelier Sadie Harris, when things turned hot fast. Meeting a year later, he's shocked by the secret she's kept. Can things remain professional when the attraction's still there?

#2847 THE PERFECT FAKE DATE
Billionaires of Boston • by Naima Simone
Learning he's the secret heir to a business mogul, Kenan Rhodes has a lot to prove. He asks best friend and lingerie designer Eve Burke to work with him, and she agrees...if he'll help her sharpen her dating skills. Soon, fake dates lead to sexy nights...

#2848 RETURN OF THE RANCHER
by Janice Maynard
After their passionate whirlwind marriage ended five years ago, India Lamont is shocked when her mysterious ex, businessman Farris Quinn, invites her to his Wyoming ranch to help his ailing mother. The attraction's still there...and so are his long-held secrets...

#2849 THE BAD BOY EXPERIMENT
The Bourbon Brothers • by Reese Ryan
When real estate developer Cole Abbott's high school crush returns to town, she has him rethinking his no-commitment stance. So when newly divorced Renee Lockwood proposes a no-strings fling, he's in. As things turn serious, will this fiery love affair turn into forever?

#2850 TALL, DARK AND OFF LIMITS
Men of Maddox Hill • by Shannon McKenna
Responsible for Maddox Hill Architecture's security, Zack Austin takes his job very seriously. Unfortunately, his best friend and the CEO's sister, Ava Maddox, has a talent for finding trouble. When Ava needs his help, he must ignore every bit of their undeniable attraction...

SPECIAL EXCERPT FROM

(H) HARLEQUIN
DESIRE

*Learning he's the secret heir to a business mogul,
Kenan Rhodes has a lot to prove. His best friend,
lingerie designer Eve Burke, agrees to work with him...
if he'll help her sharpen her dating skills.
Soon, fake dates lead to sexy nights...*

Read on for a sneak peek of
The Perfect Fake Date,
by USA TODAY *bestselling author Naima Simone.*

The corridor ended, and he stood in front of another set of towering doors. Kenan briefly hesitated, then grasped the handle, opened the doors and slipped through to the balcony beyond. The cool April night air washed over him. The calendar proclaimed spring had arrived, but winter hadn't yet released its grasp over Boston, especially at night. But he welcomed the chilled breeze over his face, let it seep beneath the confines of his tuxedo to the hot skin below. Hoped it could cool the embers of his temper...the still-burning coals of his hurt.

"For someone who is known as the playboy of Boston society, you sure will ditch a party in a hot second." Slim arms slid around him, and he closed his eyes in pain and pleasure as the petite, softly curved body pressed to his back. "All I had to do was follow the trail of longing glances from the women in the hall to figure out where you'd gone."

He snorted. "Do you lie to your mama with that mouth? There was hardly anyone out there."

"Fine," Eve huffed. "So I didn't go with the others and watched all of that go down with your parents and brother. I waited until you left the ballroom and went after you."

"Why?" he rasped.

He felt rather than witnessed her shrug. The same with the small kiss she pressed to the middle of his shoulder blades. He locked his muscles, forcing his head not to fall back. Ordering his throat to imprison the moan scrabbling up from his chest. Commanding his dick to stand down.

"Because you needed me," she said.

So simple. So goddamn true.

He did need her. Her friendship. Her body.

Her heart.

But since he could only have one of those, he'd take it. With a woman like her—generous, sweet, beautiful of body and spirit—even part of her was preferable to none of her. And if he dared to profess his true feelings, that was exactly what he would be left with. None of her. Their friendship would be ruined, and she was too important to him to risk losing her.

Carefully, he turned and wrapped her in his embrace, shielding her from the night air. Convincing himself if this was all he could have of her—even if it meant Gavin would have all of her—then he would be okay, he murmured, "You're really going to have to remove 'rescue best friend' off your résumé. For one, it's beginning to get too time-consuming. And two, the cape clashes with your gown."

She chuckled against his chest, tipping her head back to smile up at him. He curled his fingers against her spine, but that didn't prevent the ache to trace that sensual bottom curve.

"Where would be the fun in that? You're stuck with me, Kenan. And I'm stuck with you. Friends forever."

Friends.

The sweet sting of that knife buried between his ribs.

"Always, sweetheart."

Don't miss what happens next in
The Perfect Fake Date *by Naima Simone,*
the next book in the Billionaires of Boston series!

Available January 2022 wherever
Harlequin Desire books and ebooks are sold.

Harlequin.com